THE HORSESHOE TRILOGIES

Full of Hope

by
Lucy Daniels

HYPERION
New York

Text copyright © 2004 by Working Partners Limited
Cover illustration copyright © 2004 by Tristan Elwell

The Horseshoe Trilogies and the Volo colophon are trademarks of Disney Enterprises, Inc.
Volo® is a registered trademark of Disney Enterprises, Inc.

Printed in the United States of America

First U.S. edition, 2004
1 3 5 7 9 10 8 6 4 2

This book is set in 12.5-point Life Roman.
ISBN 0-7868-1751-8

Visit www.hyperionbooksforchildren.com

Special thanks to Linda Chapman

CHAPTER ONE

Josie Grace patted Hope's neck, enjoying the sound of hooves thudding on dry summer grass as the gray mare trotted smoothly around the field.

"Josie!"

Glancing around, Josie saw her mom standing by the field gate.

"Can you bring Hope over now, please?" Mary Grace called. "Bailey's ready to ride."

"Coming," Josie shouted back. Slowing Hope to a walk, she ruffled the mare's wiry, gray mane. "Good girl," she praised. "Now that you're warmed up, it's time to go and meet another new rider." Almost as if she understood what Josie had said,

Hope started walking eagerly toward the gate, her ears pricked.

Josie smiled. Friendship House—a center where physically challenged children came for their vacations—was the perfect new home for Hope. Up until a few months ago, the gray mare had belonged to Josie's mom, and Josie had ridden her all the time. But then Josie's mom had been forced to close her small riding school, and although Josie had been able to keep her beloved Charity, Hope and the other horse, Faith, had had to be sold. Faith had been bought by Josie's friend, Jill Atterbury, and Hope had gone to the center. With her straight nose, small eyes, and broad back, Hope wasn't the prettiest horse in the world, but she was very kind and patient and she seemed to enjoy living at Friendship House. The children there all adored her—and she adored them back.

Yes, Josie thought. If Mom and I can't have Hope, then this is definitely the best place for her to be.

As they reached the gate, Josie saw Pat, one of the helpers at Friendship House, walking toward the field with a girl who looked about nine years old. The girl had thick, dark brown hair cut in a short bob around her heart-shaped face. She was walking slowly using a metal walker, and her movements looked stiff and awkward.

Josie guessed she must be Bailey Williams, a girl with cerebral palsy who had just arrived at Friendship House. Josie had met other children with cerebral palsy and knew that their brains had problems getting messages to their muscles, which meant they often had a hard time walking. Some of the children she had met used wheelchairs all the time. But they were often very good at riding. Being on a horse seemed to help their muscles relax and their coordination improve.

Mrs. Grace went over to meet Bailey and Pat. She and Josie were there to give Bailey a riding lesson. For most of the summer, twelve-year-old Zoe had been giving the children rides on Hope while she stayed with her grandmother Joan, the cook at Friendship House. Two weeks ago, Zoe had returned home to her mom, and so Mrs. Grace had offered to supervise rides when she could spare the time. Josie always tried to go with her. It meant she got to see Hope, and she really liked helping the children. They all seemed to love riding, and it was great to see them improve with each ride they had.

Josie smiled as Bailey approached. "Hi," she said, dismounting.

The younger girl didn't smile back. Her large, gray eyes looked wary.

"Bailey, this is Hope," said Mrs. Grace. "And my daughter, Josie."

Bailey didn't say anything.

Mrs. Grace opened the gate. "Come and say hello. Hope's very friendly."

Not looking at Mrs. Grace, Bailey walked into the field. She stopped just in front of Hope and reached her palm out toward the horse. Hope blew softly on Bailey's fingers. A smile lit up Bailey's distrustful face.

"Hello, girl," she whispered to Hope.

Hope raised her muzzle to Bailey's face and breathed in and out. Bailey's eyes glowed. "You're beautiful," she murmured, stroking Hope's cheek.

Josie felt a rush of warmth toward the younger girl. Anyone who thought Hope was beautiful was all right by her!

Hope snorted softly as if she knew she was being praised and nuzzled Bailey's dark hair with her soft lips. It looked as though the two of them were definitely going to get along.

"Well, let's get you mounted, Bailey," Mary Grace said.

Bailey jumped, as if startled. It was as though she'd been so engrossed in the horse she had forgotten that Mrs. Grace, Josie, and Pat were there.

"This is Bailey's helmet," said Pat, holding out a hard hat.

Mrs. Grace helped Bailey put the hat on. "Josie, can you lead Hope to the mounting block, please?"

It took a little while for Bailey to climb the steps of the mounting block and get on to Hope's back, but Hope stood without moving, her white-gray ears flicking back and forth as a fly buzzed around her head.

Josie's heart swelled with pride as she looked at the patient mare. Hope really was a horse in a million.

"Okay, let's get you into the right position," Mrs. Grace said once Bailey had mounted. "You've ridden before, haven't you?"

Bailey nodded. "I used to have lessons twice a week," she said as Mrs. Grace gently began to guide her stiff muscles into the correct position. "But then we moved and my mom and dad couldn't find a riding school nearby that would give me lessons. I haven't ridden for a while."

"Well, I'm sure you'll remember everything very quickly," Mrs. Grace told her. "But we'll start slowly until you get confident again. Josie will walk on one side of you and Pat on the other while I lead Hope."

"Hope's really fun to ride," Josie said reassuringly. "She'll take good care of you, Bailey."

To Josie's surprise, instead of looking comforted, a flash of irritation crossed Bailey's face. She opened her mouth as if she were going to say something, but then she shut it again and stared down at Hope's neck. Mrs. Grace was busy with Hope's reins and didn't notice.

"Are you ready?" Mrs. Grace asked. "Then why don't you walk on?" she said, when Bailey nodded. Bailey squeezed with her legs, and Hope moved obediently forward.

At first, Bailey looked tense, but after a few minutes she seemed to pick up the rhythm of Hope's smooth walk, and Josie saw some of the stiffness leave her. Bailey's legs started to stretch down, and her fingers relaxed on the reins.

"That's it, just let yourself feel the movement," Mrs. Grace instructed as they walked around the field. "Try and push your heels down toward the ground."

Compared to some of the other children Josie had helped, Bailey had really good balance. She sat still in the saddle, her body following Hope's movement. After three loops around the field, Pat stopped by the gate, leaving Josie as Bailey's only side-walker. Mrs. Grace took the lead rope off and let Bailey steer Hope by herself.

"You're doing great," Mrs. Grace praised as Bailey changed the rein. "Would you like to try a trot?"

For the first time, Bailey spoke up eagerly. "Yes, please!"

"All right! Josie, can you hold on to Bailey's leg, please?"

"Sure . . ." Josie started to say, but Bailey interrupted.

"I don't need her to. I used to trot all the time when I rode before."

Mrs. Grace smiled. "I'm sure you did. But it has been a while since you trotted last, so, I'd like Josie to hold on to you to start with. Okay?"

Bailey looked annoyed, but she nodded.

"Shorten your reins and get ready to trot," said Mrs. Grace, giving Bailey plenty of time to prepare herself for the quicker gate. "And trot!" she called when Bailey was ready.

Josie saw Bailey touch Hope with her heels, and Hope sped up obediently. The gray mare's trot was steady and even, but Bailey seemed to find it difficult to find the rhythm. She bounced around awkwardly and Josie had to hang on tight to the girl's leg to keep her from coming right out of the saddle.

"I think we'd better walk," said Mrs. Grace.

Josie glanced at Bailey's face. The younger girl looked disappointed. "Good job," Josie told her encouragingly. "You did really great."

"No I didn't!" Bailey burst out angrily. "I wasn't good at all!"

"Hey, don't be so hard on yourself, Bailey," Mrs. Grace said calmly. "Remember, you haven't ridden for a year."

"And trotting *is* really bumpy," Josie added.

"We'll do a little more walking," Mrs. Grace continued. "Then we can try a trot again."

By the end of the lesson, Bailey had trotted four more times. With each attempt, she had improved, but she still looked frustrated.

Seeing the unhappiness on her face, Josie tried to imagine what it must be like to get on a horse again after not riding for a year.

It must feel so strange, she thought.

"I think that's enough for today," Mrs. Grace said after twenty minutes. "We don't want to do too much on your first day back, Bailey."

"You did so well," Josie praised.

Bailey shot her an angry look. It was just a flicker in her eyes, but Josie still felt shocked. The other children she helped with were usually cheerful and happy after their rides.

Just then, Pat came to meet them with Bailey's walker. "That looked good, Bailey. Do you want to use your walker? If you're feeling tired, I can go and get your wheelchair."

"No. I don't need my wheelchair," Bailey said quickly. "I'll be fine with the walker."

"Let's get you down, then," said Mrs. Grace,

helping her dismount while Josie held Hope's reins.

"Thank you for the lesson," Bailey muttered when she was back on the ground.

"My pleasure," Mrs. Grace told her warmly. "And if the physiotherapist agrees, you can have another lesson tomorrow."

"Really? Thank you!" Bailey put her hand out and patted Hope. "I like Hope."

Hope softly pushed her head against Bailey's chest. Bailey rubbed her ears. "You're such a good girl, aren't you?" she murmured. Hope snorted appreciatively, leaving a trail of foam over Bailey's blue T-shirt. Bailey let out a squeak.

Josie started to pull Hope's head away, but then she saw that Bailey was grinning.

"Thanks a lot, Hope," said the younger girl, rubbing the horse's nose. "That will teach me to say nice things about you."

Hope's dark eyes twinkled mischievously, and she nudged Bailey with her muzzle again. Bailey giggled.

"Let's go, Bailey," said Pat. "There's an art class about to start."

The happiness faded instantly from Bailey's eyes. "I don't want to go."

"But the art classes are fun," Pat said in surprise. "It'll be a good way to meet the other kids."

"I just want to go to my room," Bailey said. "I'm really . . . I'm tired."

Pat hesitated. "Well, if you're sure."

Bailey nodded. "I'm sure."

"I'll see you tomorrow, Bailey," Mrs. Grace said. "Come on, Josie. Let's get Hope untacked." Bailey gave Hope one last pat and then Mrs. Grace led the horse away.

Josie followed her mom to the stable. Friendship House had once been an inn, and the stables were old, with dark, mossy tiles on the roof. Josie loved them. Sometimes when she was grooming Hope she liked to try to imagine all the horses that had been stabled there over the years. She wished there were still enough horses there to fill the stalls, but unless she rode Charity over to Friendship House, Hope's was the only head that looked out over the stall doors. Jack and Jill, the donkeys, lived outside, with a cozy shelter for the times when it rained.

"Bailey got right back into it," Mrs. Grace remarked as they reached Hope's stall.

"Yeah, she really seemed to like Hope," Josie

agreed, remembering how the younger girl's face had lit up when Hope had nuzzled her. "But she didn't say that much to us, did she?"

"She's probably feeling a little shy," said Mrs. Grace. "After all, she just got here. I'm sure it's going to take some time to get used to everything."

Josie nodded. She realized it must have been hard for Bailey to come to a new place where she didn't know anyone.

"Now, let's get Hope untacked," Mrs. Grace said. "I told Liz I'd stay around to give a few more lessons after lunch. We'll leave Hope in her stall for now."

"I'll go and get some hay for her," Josie offered.

When she returned with the hay she found her mom had untacked Hope and was cleaning out the stall, putting the dirty straw into an old muck bucket. Hope was standing quietly in the corner, nibbling on some leftover bits of hay. Her eyes were bright and her flea-bitten gray coat had a healthy sheen. Josie smiled as she let herself into the stall. It was good to see Hope looking so well. Not long ago Hope had had a serious case of pneumonia, but she had fought off the illness and now she was back to her old self.

At the sight of the fresh hay, Hope's ears pricked forward and she grabbed a mouthful before Josie could even put it down. "Hang on, you greedy thing," Josie laughed. Still, she was glad to see that Hope's appetite was back.

"Remember to put the hay where she can get to it easily," Mrs. Grace reminded her.

"I know, Mom," said Josie, placing the hay under Hope's feed bucket. Hope continued to pull at it, causing bits of hay to fall into Josie's wavy auburn hair.

"And add a little water . . ."

". . . So she doesn't eat any dust," Josie finished as she walked out of the stall. She looked at her mom with a mix of humor and exasperation. "I've been doing this since I was five, Mom! I think I know how to do it by now."

"Sorry, sweetie." Mary Grace gave a rueful smile. "I guess I just miss being around horses."

"But we've still got Charity at home," Josie pointed out. "And you ride Connie." Connie was a black mare who had used to be boarded at their old barn. Mrs. Grace had stayed in touch with her owner and still rode Connie at least once a week.

Josie saw a look of sadness cross her mother's face. "You should get another job with horses, Mom," she suggested.

"But what?" Mrs. Grace replied doubtfully. "There aren't that many opportunities for riding teachers around here. Lonsdale Stables is fully staffed, and I can't see any jobs opening up in the near future."

The sound of footsteps outside the barn interrupted their conversation. They both turned as a young woman with short, light brown hair appeared in the doorway. It was Liz Tallant, Friendship House's manager and owner.

"I just thought I'd come and see how Bailey Williams's first ride went," Liz said.

"It went great," said Mrs. Grace. Josie gave Hope one last pat and joined her mother and Liz. "She seemed a bit frustrated that she was out of practice, but I think she'll improve quickly."

"That's good to hear," said Liz. "Her parents told me she's completely horse crazy. In fact, they said it was only when she found out she could ride here that she agreed to come. It's the first time she's ever been away from home."

"She did seem a little shy," Josie said.

"Well, she hasn't joined in with the other children much," Liz admitted. "But maybe riding will bring her out of her shell."

Mrs. Grace nodded. "It's wonderful what being around horses can do for someone. I think it's a shame that there aren't more riding schools around here that cater to children with physical challenges."

As Liz nodded, an idea popped into Josie's head—a fantastic, amazing idea. "I've got it!" she gasped. "Why don't you start a riding school for these kids, Mom? It could be located here at Friendship House. There's plenty of room, and children like Bailey could come on weekends or after school! You could run it and then you'd be working with horses again."

She saw her mom's eyes light up. "A riding school here. That *would* be great!"

Josie looked quickly over at Liz. But to her dismay, Liz was shaking her head. "It's a wonderful idea, and I would love to have a riding school here," she said sadly. "But it's just not possible. There's no way we could afford to set up something like that right now."

"But it would take just a few more horses," Josie

said, her mind buzzing as she imagined telling her best friends Anna and Jill all about it. "We could raise the money to buy them!"

"It's not just buying them, though," Liz pointed out. "It's the upkeep. Feeding them and shoeing them, and there would be your mom's wages, not to mention the insurance needed to run that type of business."

Josie's happiness fizzled.

"Right now our funds are at an all-time low," Liz continued. "I just had part of the roof repaired and it really ate into our savings."

"Are things going to be okay, Liz?" Mary Grace asked with concern.

"I really don't know," Liz replied. "We'll get by as long as nothing else major needs fixing soon. If it does, well . . ." She hesitated. "I'm not sure what will happen then."

"I didn't realize things were that bad," said Mrs. Grace.

Liz sighed. "I have to admit, things have never looked as rocky as they do now. If we don't get some more money soon, I might have to think about closing."

"Friendship House can't close down!" Josie exclaimed.

"That's what I keep telling myself," said Liz. She looked at their worried faces and forced a smile. "I'm sure things will work out. They usually do. Just keep your fingers crossed that nothing else goes wrong around here." She took a deep breath. "Anyway, I'd better get going. I'll see you both later. Thanks again for helping Bailey, Mary."

Josie stared after Liz as she walked back toward the house. She couldn't believe it. Friendship House was important to many children. And it was Hope's new home! They *couldn't* let it close!

CHAPTER TWO

"We've got to do something to help Liz," declared Anna Marshall at lunch that day. "Friendship House can't shut down."

"I know," Josie said, agreeing with her best friend. Anna had arrived at Friendship House with her mom, Lynne Marshall, who taught art classes to the children there. As soon as Josie saw her, she had filled her in on Liz's news. Now the two of them were sitting outside Hope's barn soaking up the sun. Their lunches sat in front of them, but Josie had lost her appetite thinking about the dreadful news.

Anna pushed a strand of her glossy, straight, black hair behind her ear. "We need to raise some money," she decided.

"How are we going to do that?" Josie asked, moving out of the sun. Her pale skin burned easily, whereas Anna, with her olive complexion, could stay out in the sun all day. Usually Josie was a little envious, but today she had more troubling thoughts to deal with.

"I have no clue." Anna took a bite of her cheese sandwich. "How about we sell things at a yard sale?"

Josie shook her head. "No good. Mom and Dad cleared out all our old junk when we moved, and didn't your mom just give a load of stuff to Mrs. Atterbury for her yard sale?"

Anna's forehead creased. "Oh, yeah. I forgot about that."

"We could make things and sell them," Josie suggested.

Anna grinned. "Sure, because we're both so good at making things!"

"I guess you're right," Josie said with a sigh. "I made a clay dog in art last year and when I brought it home, Dad thought it was a hippo. A yard sale wouldn't raise much money, anyway," Josie continued. "And it looks like Liz needs a lot."

Suddenly, Hope shifted in her stall. She stamped

the floor with her hoof and stretched her neck over the stall door until her lips quivered against Josie's hair. Josie reached up and gave her a little pat. "We need to find a way of getting lots of money—enough so that Liz can do the repairs she needs *and* start a riding school. That way Friendship House would become so popular that it couldn't possibly close!"

"If only Liz could win the lottery or something," Anna said.

Josie reached up and scratched Hope's neck. "That would be perfect!"

"Not that realistic, though," said Anna.

Josie nodded her head in agreement. "It looks like we need to keep thinking of ideas."

Josie racked her brain for the rest of that day and night trying to think of something they could do, but by the next morning she still hadn't come up with anything.

"Is Bailey having another lesson today?" she asked her mom as they pulled up outside Friendship House.

"I'm not sure. I've got to talk to Karen, the physiotherapist, and see what she says," Mrs. Grace replied. "She's keeping an eye on Bailey to make sure riding isn't making her muscles any stiffer." She got out of the car. "I'm going to find her now. Can you bring Hope in from the field?"

"Sure," Josie replied, heading off around the honey-colored building that made up the main part of Friendship House. The sun was shining and the sky was a brilliant blue. Perfect summer weather, thought Josie, glad that she wasn't stuck in school on such a hot day.

When she arrived at the field, Hope wasn't there and Josie glanced toward the stables wondering if Sid, the gardener who helped look after Hope and the donkeys, had brought Hope in.

Josie walked over to Hope's stable. The mare's outer door was shut, but Josie couldn't remember if she had left it open the night before when she had turned Hope out. As she got closer to Hope's stall, she heard a girl's voice from inside. "You're the best horse in the whole world, Hope, and soon we'll be able to do all sorts of fun things. We'll trot and canter and maybe we'll even get to go out for a ride in the woods."

Josie peeked over the door. Hope was tied up to one wall and Bailey was standing beside her, leaning on her walker with one hand and holding a brush in the other.

As Josie watched, Hope turned her head and gently nuzzled Bailey's shoulder.

Bailey smiled. "You like me, don't you, girl? You don't care that—"

Suddenly, Hope noticed Josie. Her ears pricked up and she whickered a greeting.

Bailey jumped and nearly lost her grip on the walker.

Josie felt herself turning red. She knew it looked as though she'd been listening in on Bailey's special moment with Hope, but she really hadn't meant to spy on them. Hope and Bailey had just looked so happy that she hadn't wanted to interrupt. "Hi," she said awkwardly.

Bailey looked over at her with annoyance. "What are you doing here?"

Josie let herself into the stall. "I was coming to groom Hope, but you seem to be doing a great job," she said, trying to make the younger girl feel comfortable.

Bailey looked at Hope's muddy coat. "Not really. I hardly got any of the mud off."

"Well, *I* think you're doing great," Josie said encouragingly.

Bailey frowned but didn't say anything more.

"Would you like some help?" Josie asked.

"Whatever," Bailey muttered.

Josie was taken aback. Bailey hadn't sounded shy. She had sounded rude and unfriendly. Not knowing quite what to say, Josie fetched another brush from the brush box and went to Hope's other side.

She and Bailey worked on the horse without speaking.

After a few minutes, Pat looked over the stall door. "Are you all right, Bailey?" She saw Josie. "Oh, hi, Josie. I didn't realize you were in here. I hope you don't mind that I brought Hope in. Bailey really wanted to groom her."

"That's fine," Josie answered.

"Hope's such a good girl," Pat smiled. "I just had to go and help one of the other kids get a ball out of a hedge, but I knew Bailey would be perfectly fine all on her own."

Josie smiled. "Hope's a big softie. Bailey can groom her whenever she wants." She glanced over at Bailey. To her surprise, the younger girl was scowling.

"Do you mind if I leave you for ten minutes or so?" asked Pat. "Then I'll come back and see how you three are doing."

"No problem," Josie replied.

After Pat left, an uneasy silence fell over the stall. Josie searched for something to say. "Are you looking forward to riding Hope again?" she finally asked, trying to make the atmosphere less awkward.

Bailey gave the briefest of nods and pointedly turned her back on Josie. Josie felt a flash of irritation at the girl's rudeness. None of the other kids had ever behaved like that. Even the ones who were really shy would usually smile at her and act excited to see her. Why was Bailey being so difficult?

Suddenly, Hope shifted her position slightly and her hindquarters swung toward Josie while her shoulder knocked against Bailey's walker.

"Whoa!" Josie and Bailey both said at almost the same time.

Hope stopped moving.

"Good girl," Josie said. She hurried around to Bailey's side and pushed Hope's shoulder away. "You have to be more careful around Bailey," she gently told the mare.

Bailey glared at Josie. "No, she doesn't! I don't need special treatment! And I can get her to move over on my own. I don't need *your* help."

Josie had had enough. "Fine!" she snapped in frustration. "In that case, I guess you don't need my help grooming her."

Stuffing her brush into the box, she headed to the door, but just as she reached it, she saw her mom coming.

"How's Hope?" Mrs. Grace asked. "All groomed and ready?"

Josie's anger quickly faded. "Um, not quite," she stammered, feeling herself start to blush. She couldn't believe she had snapped at Bailey like that. She glanced over her shoulder at the girl. Bailey quickly looked away.

"Hello, Bailey," said Mrs. Grace, coming into the stall. "Liz said you were here. I've got some good news for you. Karen is so pleased with how your muscles responded to riding yesterday that she's suggested you ride every day. How does that sound?"

A smile lit up Bailey's sulky face. "Great!" she exclaimed.

"I thought you'd be pleased. Let's finish getting

Hope groomed and then you can get on," said Mrs. Grace. "Grab a brush, Josie, and we'll all do it together."

Twenty minutes later, Hope was tacked up and Bailey was riding her around the ring.

Josie walked beside Hope while Bailey steered her. Even though she had calmed down, she was still feeling guilty about her earlier outburst. Bailey hadn't said a word to her since.

"Prepare to halt," Mrs. Grace called out. "And halt!"

Bailey brought Hope to a standstill. Josie patted Hope's warm neck.

"Very good, Bailey," Mrs. Grace praised. "Would you like to try a trot again?"

Bailey nodded eagerly.

"All right, then," said Mrs. Grace, going over to the fence and picking up a lunge line and a long whip. "Josie, can you take off Hope's reins, please?"

Josie nodded and started to unfasten the reins at the bit.

"You're taking the reins off?" Bailey asked, a tremor of fear creeping into her voice.

"You don't need any reins, because I'll be steering Hope," Mrs. Grace explained. "I think you should try trotting on the lunge line today. You'll be able to concentrate more on your position in the saddle."

"But . . . but I don't want to be lunged!" Bailey cried.

Josie's mom looked surprised. "Why not?"

"I've ridden before!" Bailey exclaimed. "I don't need to go on a lunge line! That's for beginners and I can already ride," she said stubbornly.

"I know that," Mrs. Grace told her, studying her angry face. "I hope you don't think that I'm suggesting the lunge line because of anything having to do with your ability, Bailey," she said softly.

Josie saw Bailey's eyes narrow.

"Lunging is a good way to improve your seat," Mrs. Grace told her. "It doesn't matter how good you are or how long you've ridden. Lots of top riders have lessons on a lunge line. Please, will you just give it a try? I really think it will help."

Bailey hesitated. "I guess so," she finally said, reluctantly.

Mrs. Grace smiled. "Good."

Josie felt a rush of relief as her mom attached the lunge line to Hope's bridle.

"You can keep your stirrups for now," Mrs. Grace told Bailey. "But really concentrate on letting yourself follow Hope's movement. Josie will walk beside you in case you lose your balance. Off you go." She moved away and flicked the whip at Hope's hindquarters. "Walk on, Hope."

At the end of the long lunge line, Hope began to walk in a large circle around Mrs. Grace. Josie walked beside Bailey's outside leg, not holding on to her but close enough that she could help if Bailey had a problem. It felt very familiar. When her mom had run the riding school, Josie had used to help with the lunge lessons. She watched as Bailey relaxed into the saddle.

Soon Bailey was trotting, her body rising and falling in time to Hope's strides.

"Good job. Take a break," Mrs. Grace said as she slowed Hope to a walk. Josie wiped her forehead with the back of her hand. "And once you have your breath back, I think we should try it without stirrups."

"Without stirrups?" Bailey echoed, looking worried.

Mrs. Grace nodded. "Yes. Slip your feet out so Josie can take them off the saddle. You'll be more comfortable if they're out of the way."

"But I have never ridden without stirrups before," Bailey protested.

"There's a first time for everything," Mrs. Grace said, smiling. "Come on," she added, seeing Bailey's alarmed and hesitant expression. "You're not going to tell me you can't do it, are you?"

Bailey swallowed but rose to the challenge. "No. I can do it."

"Now that's what I like to hear," said Mrs. Grace.

Josie moved toward the saddle. "Don't worry," she said to Bailey as she eased the stirrup leather off its metal hook. "Hope's got such a broad back that she's really comfy to ride without stirrups."

Bailey just scowled and remained silent.

Josie decided to give up trying to be nice. She moved to the other side and yanked off the stirrup.

Once the saddle was ready, Mrs. Grace started lunging Bailey again. Josie could tell that Bailey was anxious, but she was soon trotting around without reins or stirrups. And much to Josie's relief, her mom said that she could wait by the gate instead of running beside Hope and Bailey.

Josie went and sat on the gate to watch.

"There, see?" said Mrs. Grace as Bailey slowed to a walk after trotting two complete circles on her own. "I knew you could do it."

A broad smile broke out on Bailey's face and she reached forward to pat Hope's neck.

"Let's bring Hope in," Mrs. Grace said. "I think you've done enough for one day."

Bailey rode Hope over to the gate. Josie jumped down from her perch and took the horse's head while Mrs. Grace helped Bailey dismount.

"Thank you," Bailey said happily to Mrs. Grace as her feet came to rest on the grass.

"My pleasure," Mrs. Grace replied, taking Bailey's walker and handing it to her. "I wish all riders were as determined as you, Bailey. You did great today."

Bailey's eyes glowed. "I had so much fun! I like taking lessons with you, Mrs. Grace. You're a really good teacher."

Mrs. Grace smiled. "Why, thank you, Bailey."

"Can I help put Hope away?" Bailey eagerly asked. "I could groom her some more."

"I've got to go to see Liz," Mrs. Grace told her. "But I'm sure Josie would love some help."

Josie saw Bailey's face fall.

Mrs. Grace didn't seem to notice the change in Bailey's expression. "You don't mind taking Hope in, do you, Josie?"

"No problem," Josie replied, her heart sinking. Much as she loved spending time with Hope, it wasn't going to be fun if Bailey was there being mean. Forcing a smile, she turned toward the girl. "Come on, Bailey. You can lead Hope."

Bailey took the reins in one hand and began slowly to lead Hope up to the stable. Hope walked patiently beside her, waiting when she needed to, never pushing or barging.

"You're doing well," Josie said, encouraging Bailey as they got closer to the stable.

Bailey looked at her as if she were crazy. "I'm just leading her. It's no big deal!"

Josie took a deep breath. Why did Bailey seem so determined to be mad at her?

CHAPTER THREE

As they reached the stable, Pat came out to meet them. "Should we go and find some of the others, Bailey?" she asked sweetly.

Bailey shook her head. "Mrs. Grace said I could help with Hope."

"A music class is about to start," Pat told her. "It will be fun."

"I don't want to go to a music class," Bailey insisted. "I want to stay here."

Pat frowned. "Bailey, you won't make any friends if you don't join any of the classes."

"So?" Bailey muttered. She moved her walker around and began to try to undo Hope's girth.

"Do you want me to help?" Josie offered, realizing the girl was struggling.

"No!" Bailey said sharply. "I can manage!"

Josie glanced at Pat. The older woman shrugged. "Well, if you're not coming in, Bailey, I'm going back to the house," she said. "Can you stay here, Josie?"

Josie nodded. "Sure, no problem."

Pat turned and left. Josie watched Bailey fumble with the girth but bit her tongue. She didn't want to be snapped at again. It took four attempts, but eventually Bailey got the girth undone and a satisfied smile flitted across her face.

"Could you take the saddle off, please?" she said to Josie in an almost friendly voice.

Josie took the saddle and hung it over the stall door.

"Can I clean it?" Bailey asked. "I used to clean my tack at my old riding school after every lesson."

"I guess so," Josie said in surprise. Cleaning tack wasn't the most fun part of riding. "I'll . . . uh . . . go and get some water."

She got a bucket from the tack room and took it to the hose to get some water. Looking out the door as the bucket filled up, she saw Bailey stroking

Hope's face and talking quietly to her. Hope's eyes were half closed in bliss.

Josie was confused. Bailey might be difficult to get along with at times, but she couldn't be all bad. Not when she obviously loved horses—and Hope in particular—so much. Josie sighed. Maybe she should try to give her another chance.

Turning off the hose, Josie went back to the stall.

"Here you go," she said, smiling as she put the bucket down. "I'll go and get the rest of the stuff."

She brought out the saddle soap, a couple of sponges, and the wooden saddle horse. Taking everything outside, she put the saddle on the wooden structure at a height that Bailey could reach. Then she put the saddle soap close by so that Bailey wouldn't have to lean over each time she needed it.

"How's that?" she asked.

"Good." Bailey's eyes met Josie's. "Thanks." She sounded as though she meant it, and Josie was amazed to see a smile catch the corners of her mouth.

Encouraged, Josie smiled back. "No problem. I'll do the bridle while you do the saddle."

They had just started cleaning the tack when they heard the sound of voices. Josie glanced up. Pat was heading toward them with two children beside her, a boy with dark, curly hair and a girl with blond pigtails. Josie recognized them at once. Matthew and Katie had been at Friendship House for a week. Although neither of them had ridden before, they loved horses and came down to the stables a lot to see Hope. Matthew wore braces on both legs, and Katie had a limp, because one of her legs was shorter than the other.

"I found some more helpers for you, Josie," Pat called. "When Matthew and Katie heard that Bailey was here, they wanted to come out, too. Is that all right?"

"Fine," Josie replied agreeably.

"What are you doing?" asked Matthew, looking curiously at the water and sponges.

"We're cleaning Hope's tack," Josie replied. "Would you like to help?"

Matthew and Katie nodded eagerly. As Josie handed them sponges, it occurred to her that this might be a good way for Bailey to start making friends. "Katie, why don't you help me with the bridle? And Matthew, you can help Bailey with the saddle."

"Sure . . ." Matthew started to say, but he was interrupted by Bailey.

"I don't want any help!" Bailey shouted, stepping away from the saddle.

"Bailey," Pat said firmly. "It'll be fun with Matthew and Katie helping."

"I changed my mind. I'm going inside," Bailey said abruptly. Grabbing her walker, she began to walk away.

Josie followed. "Bailey, please stay," she pleaded. "Matthew and Katie are really nice. And they like horses. You guys could be friends."

"I don't want friends," Bailey said. With a scowl, she continued back to the house.

Josie stared after her for a moment and then went back to the others. Katie and Matthew looked confused. "Where did Bailey go?" Katie asked.

Josie shrugged. "I think she wanted to go to her room."

"Can we still help?" Matthew asked anxiously.

Josie smiled. Their enthusiasm was contagious. "Of course." But she couldn't stop thinking about

Bailey. How could the girl be so loving toward Hope but so angry with people?

"I just don't get it," she said later that afternoon as she and her mother drove home for some lunch. "Bailey seemed happy cleaning the tack, but as soon as Pat turned up with Matthew and Katie, she left and went to her room."

Mrs. Grace sighed. "I think she's probably having trouble settling in. Liz was saying she doesn't seem to want to socialize with anyone at Friendship House—not the other children, not even the helpers. When she isn't with Hope she just stays in her room."

"Why?" Josie persisted. "I know you said yesterday that she might be shy, but she doesn't seem *that* shy to me."

Mrs. Grace nodded. "I know," she said, her voice thoughtful. "I'm sure there's more going on than we realize. Maybe it's self-consciousness or embarrassment that's stopping her from making any friends."

"But why would she be embarrassed?" Josie asked.

"Some people are just insecure." Mrs. Grace

sighed. "In any event, I hope she settles in soon. She's going to miss out on a lot if she refuses to make friends."

"Maybe riding will help," Josie suggested. "She's improving quickly. If she's good at it, perhaps it will make her feel more confident."

"I hope so," said her mom.

"I really wish Friendship House could have a riding school," Josie said longingly. "It would be wonderful."

Mrs. Grace nodded. "I know. It would be my dream job and I'm sure it would be a success. Not to mention the fact that it could be a very good source of income for Friendship House. The horses could be used to give lessons to outside clients, too." She heaved a big sigh. "But setting it up would be expensive, and I know Liz has a hundred other things she could do with the money right now."

She turned onto the quiet road that led to their house. "So what are your plans for this afternoon?" she asked Josie, changing the subject.

"I thought I might take Charity out for a ride," Josie answered as her mom parked in front of the house.

At first, Josie hadn't wanted to move, but she had come to love their new house and the yard that led down to the field where she kept Charity. She got out of the car and hurried over to the gate. Seeing Josie, Charity whinnied in delight and trotted over. Even though she was Hope's daughter, she was more finely built than Hope, with a very pretty dished face and large, expressive eyes.

"Hi, girl. What should we do today?" Josie asked, stroking Charity's dappled-gray neck. "Up for a ride in the woods?"

Charity rubbed her head against Josie's arm.

"I'll take that as a yes," Josie said with a grin.

Half an hour later, Josie headed into the woods. Charity walked forward eagerly, her ears pricked, and Josie felt herself begin to relax. There was nothing in the world that she liked better than riding Charity.

She patted the mare's shoulder, feeling very lucky to have a horse of her own. Josie didn't know what she would do without a horse in her life. It wasn't just owning Charity that was so great, it was everything that went with riding: taking care of her horse, spending time with her other friends who rode, and even cleaning tack! Anna; Anna's twin brother, Ben; and Jill Atterbury all loved horses. The four of them were always doing fun things together like treasure hunts, picnic rides, and horse shows. And even when they weren't doing anything special, it was great just to hang around together, catching up on all things horse-related.

Josie remembered the way Bailey had talked to Hope earlier that day. Bailey really seemed to love horses, but she didn't seem to want to share her love for horses with other people. If only there were a way to persuade her to make friends with the other kids, Josie thought. I'm sure she'd have much more fun.

The path straightened out and Charity began to pull at the bit. Josie knew she wanted to canter. "Come on, girl," she whispered, shortening the reins and leaning forward in the saddle.

Charity leaped forward and as they sped along the track, all of the thoughts that had been weighing on Josie's mind slipped away: Bailey's moodiness, her mom's desire for a job with horses, Friendship House's money problems, all disappeared as, leaning close to Charity's neck, Josie lost herself in the rhythmic drumming of hooves.

Josie stayed out for almost two hours. By the time she had cooled Charity down, fed her, and turned her out, she was *very* hungry and *very* thirsty. She walked wearily into the kitchen and poured herself a big glass of ice-cold apple juice. She had downed half of it and was just opening up a box of crackers when she heard her dad's footsteps in the front hall.

"Hi," Josie greeted him. She noticed he had a huge smile on his face. "You look like you're in a good mood."

"I am," he said. "I just got back from a meeting at school."

"Sure doesn't sound like my idea of fun," Josie teased. Her dad was the head of English and drama at a nearby school—luckily, not the one Josie went to. She loved her dad but she thought it would be really weird to be his student.

"Yes, but this was a meeting where I heard some good news," he said triumphantly.

"What good news?" Josie asked curiously.

Just then, her mom came down the stairs.

"You're back! Did you hear anything about the grant?"

"Yes!" Her dad's face stretched into an even broader grin. "And . . . we got it!"

"Rob, that's great!" Mrs. Grace said, hurrying over and hugging him.

Josie was confused. "What's great?"

"Last term I applied for a grant for our school," her dad explained. "It was to get money to update our sound, staging, and lighting systems. Well, we just heard that we were given the money. We're going to be able to revamp the entire school theater." His eyes shone. "We'll be able to do really great productions now. It will be like working in a professional theater!"

"Cool!" Josie said, going over and giving him a hug. "Congratulations, Dad."

"I bought the ingredients to make a special meal in honor of the good news," her dad said, holding up two grocery bags. "How does homemade lasagna and salad followed by strawberries and ice cream sound?"

"Great!" Josie exclaimed, her stomach growling at the mention of food. Her dad was an amazing cook and she loved all of his special meals, even if they weren't always fancy ones.

The three of them made their way to the kitchen. "It's just such good news about the grant," said Mrs. Grace.

Josie's dad nodded in agreement. "We should have applied before. There's lots of money available for educational purposes and good causes. It's just a matter of applying."

Josie stared at him. His words had caused an idea to pop into her head.

"So, there's really a lot of money available?" Josie demanded.

Looking confused, her dad nodded. "Yes. For all kinds of causes."

"Like . . ." Josie stared at him in excitement. "Like a riding school at Friendship House, for instance?"

CHAPTER FOUR

"Well?" Josie persisted. "If there *is* a lot of money available, couldn't Liz apply for a grant to start a riding school?"

"Well," said her dad, staring at her. "I don't see why not."

"Sweetie, that's a great idea!" her mom cried.

Josie glowed with pride.

Mrs. Grace looked thrilled. "I'll give the office a call first thing in the morning and find out if there is any funding available for a project like this."

"And in the meantime, we could do some research on the Web," Mr. Grace suggested. "There's a ton of information about all the different types of grants."

"Great idea, Dad!" Josie said. "I don't think I can eat until I learn more about this."

It didn't take long for Mr. Grace and Josie to find the information they needed. To Josie's delight, the office's Web site said that there were plenty of grants available for setting up or improving facilities similar to Friendship House.

"This is perfect," Josie exclaimed as they printed out the page. She brought it over to her mom. "Look!"

"I'm going to call Liz right now and tell her about this," Mrs. Grace said excitedly.

A little later, Mrs. Grace hung up the phone with a smile on her face.

"Well?" Josie asked.

"Liz thinks it's a great idea. She's going to call the grant people in the morning. And she said that if they do get the money, she would love to put me in charge of the riding program at Friendship House."

"Oh, Mom," Josie said, hugging her. "You would be running a riding school again!"

"Calm down," her mom said, laughing. "We

don't know if we even have the money yet. There's no point in getting too excited until we know more."

But Josie couldn't calm down. "I'm going to call Anna!" she said and picked up the phone. Her heart was racing as she dialed her friend's number.

"Are you kidding?" Anna gasped in disbelief when she heard the news. "That is so cool, Josie! I really hope Liz gets the money!"

Before Josie and Anna got off the phone with each other, they arranged to meet up the next day. "My mom has some more lessons to give. We can pick you up on the way," Josie said.

"Your mom's spending even more time at Friendship House than mine is!" Anna laughed.

"She loves teaching the kids," said Josie.

"This riding school just *has* to happen!" Anna declared.

"I couldn't agree with you more," Josie said with a hopeful sigh.

The next morning, as Mrs. Grace, Josie, and Anna drove to Friendship House, they talked about nothing but the riding school.

"How many horses would you need?" Anna asked Mrs. Grace.

"Probably just three, including Hope," Mrs. Grace replied. "The problem is going to be finding the right type of horse. They would need to be like Hope—quiet and patient, but also strong, with fairly broad backs. Finding horses like that isn't going to be easy. There's a big auction on Wednesday. I think I might go and see what sort of prices horses like that are going for."

"Can we come with you?" Josie asked eagerly.

"Of course," said her mom. "As long as you realize we are just looking, not buying," she added, glancing over her shoulder with a warning look at both Josie and Anna. "We can't spend a penny until we know we've got the grant."

"But, Mom," Josie pretended to protest. "You mean we can't even buy one horse?"

"Not even a little one?" Anna joined in. "I'm sure we could fit a Shetland in the trunk of the car."

Mrs. Grace raised her eyebrows. "On second thought, maybe taking you two along isn't such a good idea."

Josie grinned at her. "We'll be good, Mom. We promise."

"If you say so," said Mrs. Grace. "All right, you can come and help me look. Another big problem will be figuring out which horses won't be bothered by having wheelchairs or walkers around."

"Why don't we take a wheelchair with us?" Anna suggested.

"I know what we could do," Josie said. "We could ask Bailey if she wants to come with us." She looked at her mom. "She has a wheelchair and she's really good with horses."

"That's not a bad idea," Mrs. Grace said thoughtfully. "We'll have to check with Liz and with Bailey's parents, first."

When they arrived, they found Liz in her large, airy office by the front door. "Hi, there," she said, beaming at them. "I was just on the phone with the person in charge of grants. The woman I spoke to seemed very positive about the idea."

Josie and Anna exchanged happy looks.

"So now what do you do?" Mrs. Grace asked.

"I've got to fill out some forms. I'm actually going to drive in to town and collect them in a few minutes," Liz replied. "They sound pretty straightforward, but the woman at the office said I would need to give a breakdown of how the money will be spent." She looked over at Mrs. Grace. "I was hoping you would be able to help me with that."

"No problem," Mrs. Grace assured her. "The girls and I thought we might go to an auction on Wednesday to get an idea of how much the horses are going to cost. We also thought . . ." and she began to explain Josie's idea of inviting Bailey along.

"Great idea," said Liz. "I'll call her parents to run it by them, but I'm sure they'll say yes." She frowned. "Bailey is having a hard time settling in here. Maybe going to the sale will help."

Mrs. Grace nodded. "Speaking of which—is she having a lesson today?"

"Yes," Liz answered. "I think she's down at the stables with Hope right now. She loves that horse. Even if she's not riding or grooming her, she just likes being with her. She spends hours just petting her and standing with her."

Josie grinned. "I'm sure Hope loves all the attention. Can we tell Bailey about the auction now?"

"Let's wait until I've spoken to her parents," said

Liz. "I'm sure they'll say yes, but I'd hate her to get excited and then end up disappointing her."

Mrs. Grace nodded and looked over at Josie and Anna. "Do you two want to head down to the stable? You can help Bailey get Hope groomed and tacked up."

"So what's Bailey like?" Anna asked as she and Josie left the office and headed to the stable.

"Well, she loves horses," Josie began. "But she seems shy and weird around other kids."

Anna looked puzzled. "But all the children here are so nice!"

Josie shrugged. "I know." She stopped talking as they reached the stable because she didn't want Bailey to overhear anything.

Looking over the stall door, Josie saw Bailey standing in front of Hope, petting the gray horse's face. Hope was resting her nose against Bailey's walker. Josie hesitated. The two of them looked so peaceful that she half thought of going away and leaving them alone, but just then Bailey seemed to sense her presence and looked over.

"Hi." Josie smiled quickly as she saw the familiar, wary look spring into Bailey's eyes. "My mom will be down soon. She asked us to come and get Hope ready. Do you want some help grooming her?" Josie asked.

Bailey hesitated. "Fine," she said at last.

"I'll get the brush box," Anna offered. She raised her eyebrows at Josie as she went past. Clearly, she was surprised by Bailey's unfriendliness, in spite of Josie's warning.

While Anna was in the tack room, Josie put the halter on Hope. She really wasn't sure how to treat Bailey. If Bailey *was* feeling self-conscious about her cerebral palsy, maybe the best thing Josie could do was just ignore it and treat her like anyone else. "Here," she said matter-of-factly, handing the lead rope to Bailey. "Will you bring Hope into the aisle for me?"

A look of surprise crossed Bailey's face, but she nodded. "Sure." With the lead clasped tightly in her hand, she moved her walker slowly toward the door. "Come on, Hope," she said.

Step by step, Hope followed Bailey out of the stall. It was a squeeze to get through the door, and Bailey held Hope back while she fit her walker through. Josie forced herself not to help. Instead, she went and got an old, wooden crate to put the brush box on so that Bailey wouldn't be forced to lean down too far to get the brushes.

Anna came back with the brush box and a bucket of water just as Bailey was putting Hope on the crossties.

"Since it's such a nice day, I thought we could wash Hope's tail and legs," she said.

"Good idea," Josie agreed. "Do you want to help, Bailey?"

Bailey nodded eagerly. "I've never washed a horse's tail before."

Anna grinned at her. "Well, I'd be careful. Josie usually manages to get water everywhere!"

To Josie's amazement, Bailey actually smiled. "Sounds fun," she said quietly.

After brushing Hope off, the three of them began shampooing Hope's tail and legs.

Hope seemed rather surprised by all the helpers, but Josie knew she liked it.

"Do you like all this attention, girl?" Josie asked, as Hope nuzzled her shoulder.

"I think she does," said Anna, as she cleaned off her sponge in a bucket of fresh water.

Snorting loudly, Hope swished her tail, sending water flying. Standing near her hindquarters, Bailey shrieked as the water sprayed all over her.

"Are you all right, Bailey?" Josie asked, worried the girl might be angry, but then she saw that Bailey was grinning.

"Thanks a lot, Hope!" Bailey said, joking. "Now I'm wetter than you."

"I think we all are," said Josie, looking down at her T-shirt. She'd managed to splash water all over herself while rinsing Hope's legs.

"I don't care," Bailey said, smiling. "This is great!" Brushing the water from her jeans, she looked super-relaxed and happy.

They had just put the shampoo away when Mrs. Grace came walking into the stable. "Wow, Hope looks great," she said. "You girls have been working hard."

The three girls exchanged smiles.

"So, are you ready for your lesson, Bailey?" Mrs. Grace asked. "I think we'll do some more on the lunge line, if that's all right with you."

Bailey nodded. "Do you think I can ride without stirrups again?"

Josie felt a rush of delight. Bailey sounded so excited.

Mrs. Grace smiled at Bailey. "If you want. And I think you can try a canter today if you like."

Bailey's eyes lit up. "Yes, please!"

After helping Bailey mount Hope, Josie and Anna sat on the fence and watched her lesson. Every day, Bailey seemed to be getting stronger and more confident.

"I can't wait to tell her about the auction," Josie said to Anna as they watched.

"I know," Anna replied. "Should we go see if Liz has called Bailey's parents yet?"

"Sure," Josie said.

They jumped down from the fence and went in to the house. Liz was just coming out of her office and looked worried. "Hi, you two," she said distractedly. "Were you looking for me?"

Josie nodded. "We were just coming to see if you'd talked to Bailey's parents yet about the auction?"

"Oh, right. They said she can go," Liz replied.

"Cool!" Anna said. "It's going to be really fun and she can help us look for horses."

Liz sighed and ran a hand through her hair.

"Don't get too excited yet. I just got the forms from the grant office. They told me that I've got a good chance of getting the funding, but it might take up to three months before we see any money." She looked anxious. "And the roof seems to have sprung a new leak."

Josie felt her heart drop. Another big repair bill was the last thing Liz needed.

"I'd better get going," Liz said. "I'll see you both later."

"Bye," Josie said as Liz hurried off.

"That leak doesn't sound good," Anna said, frowning.

Josie nodded. "I know," Josie said, chewing on a fingernail nervously. She'd thought the riding school would be up and running in a month. Now, that seemed nearly impossible. She was beginning to wonder if things were going to work out after all. Liz had looked really worried.

"Come on," Anna said, interrupting her thoughts. "At least we can still go and tell Bailey about the auction."

Bailey's lesson had just ended and Pat was holding the stall door open as Mrs. Grace put Hope away.

"Hey, Bailey," Josie said walking over to Bailey, who was coming out of the tack room. "Do you want to come to an auction on Wednesday to look at some horses?"

"An auction?" Bailey's face lit up. "I'd love to!"

Anna looked over at her and grinned. "Great! It should be a lot of fun!"

"Mom, Anna, and I are going," Josie explained. "Liz might be starting a riding school and she wants to get a sense of how much the horses will cost. And it would be great if you brought your wheelchair, so that we can find out which horses are calm enough."

All the happiness drained from Bailey's face instantly. "So you just want me to come because of my wheelchair?"

Josie realized what her comment had sounded like. "Well, no, I mean not *just* because of that," she stammered. "We—"

"Forget it!" Bailey interrupted. Her eyes flashed angrily. "I don't want to go! I'm not going if you just need me because I have a wheelchair!"

She started to storm off.

"Bailey, wait!" Anna called, going after her and placing a hand gently on her arm.

Bailey swung around. "Don't touch me!" She wrenched her arm away from Anna. "Leave me alone!"

Anna stepped back when she saw the anger on Bailey's face. Bailey turned and continued into the house. For a moment neither Josie nor Anna spoke.

"Where'd Bailey go?" Pat asked in surprise when she came out of the stable.

"To the house," Josie said.

"Oh, dear," Pat said, hurrying after her.

Anna looked at Josie. "Well, that . . . um . . . didn't go too well."

"You can say that again." Josie felt awful. The words had come out all wrong. She had never meant to make Bailey feel bad. She put her hands up to her face. "What do we do? Should we go after her?"

Anna shook her head. "She probably needs some time to cool off. Maybe we should wait and find her later."

Mrs. Grace came out of the stable. "What are you two up to?"

For a moment Josie wondered if she should tell her mother what had happened, but she decided against it. "Nothing," she said calmly.

"Well, then, would you mind making a list of all the new tack, blankets, and grooming stuff we need for two more horses?" Mrs. Grace asked. "I'm going to fill in the forms tonight and drop them off at the office in the morning."

"Sure," Josie replied. She was actually glad to have something to do to take her mind off Bailey, but it didn't stop her from feeling horrible. For the first time, Bailey had seemed friendly when they were taking care of Hope. Had Josie just made the whole situation worse?

CHAPTER FIVE

By lunchtime, Josie and Anna had made their tack wish list, and they went to find Mrs. Grace. She was in the art room talking to Mrs. Marshall. The two mothers were almost as good friends as Josie and Anna were.

"Hello, you two," Mrs. Marshall said, smiling. "Have you come to help me set up for the art class? We're painting."

"Actually, we wanted to see Mom," said Josie. "We wanted to find out if there was anything else we could do to help."

"Well, I could use the help," Mrs. Marshall said, checking the clock on the wall. "The children will be here in ten minutes. I should have been getting the paints ready instead of chatting."

Mrs. Grace jumped up guiltily. "What can we do to help?"

Soon, Josie and Anna were covering each table with newspaper as Mrs. Marshall poured out paints and Mrs. Grace filled bowls with water. By the time the children arrived, each table was fully equipped with paints, brushes, paper, and water.

"I'll leave you to it," said Mrs. Grace. "Mrs. Marshall has offered to give you a ride home, Josie. I'm going to head home now and get started on those forms."

"Sounds good," Josie said. "See you later."

As her mom walked out the door, Bailey came in with Pat. She did not look happy.

Josie smiled, but Bailey ignored her. Josie's heart sank. It looked as though Bailey were still angry at Josie for her earlier comments.

"Oh, hi, Bailey," Pat said brightly. Pointing to an empty seat, she said, "You can sit next to Matthew."

Matthew smiled shyly at Bailey. "Hi."

Ignoring him, Bailey sat down with a stubborn expression on her face. "I don't want to paint. I'm no good at it."

"It doesn't matter how good you are," said Mrs. Marshall, overhearing. "Today's session is all about expressing yourself using different colors and patterns."

Bailey looked down at the desk and fiddled with the edge of the newspaper.

"Bailey's in a bad mood, isn't she?" Anna said softly as she and Josie went outside. The art room was small and she didn't want to get caught gossiping.

"I think that might be an understatement. I tried to smile at her but she wouldn't even look at me." Josie whispered back. "She definitely does not want to be in that class."

"I could tell!" said Anna. "We can try and talk to her later. Let's go see if snacks are still out in the dining room. I'm starving!"

They had just finished their snacks when they heard yelling coming from the art room.

"Do you hear that?" Anna asked.

"I wonder what's happening," Josie said.

Josie and Anna hurried up the path toward the art room. Josie suddenly recognized the shouting voice. "It's Bailey!" she gasped, breaking into a run.

Just as she reached the house, Bailey came storming out of the art room.

"Bailey! Come back!" Mrs. Marshall shouted, appearing behind her.

"No!" Bailey retorted. "I'm going to see Hope!"

Pat appeared beside Mrs. Marshall. "I'll go with her. You stay with the others," she said.

Mrs. Marshall hesitated and then saw Josie and Anna. "Girls, could you help me, please?"

Josie and Anna hurried over. They could hear the sound of someone crying in the art room. "We had a little incident," Mrs. Marshall explained. "I could really use a hand."

As they followed her into the room, Josie's eyes widened. Matthew was sitting at a desk, tears rolling down his face. His T-shirt was covered with red paint and he was being comforted by Tim, one of the other adult helpers. The other children were all whispering among themselves.

"Settle down, everyone. Everything's fine," Mrs. Marshall said. "Just continue painting."

Then she went over to Matthew and knelt down next to him. "Are you all right, Matthew?" she asked.

"My . . . my T-shirt," Matthew stammered in reply.

"It'll be fine. Tim will take you to your room and help you get cleaned up," Mrs. Marshall said, glancing at Tim, who nodded.

"Come on, Matthew," he said. "We'll have you in some clean clothes soon."

"What happened?" Anna asked her mom as Tim led Matthew out of the classroom.

"Bailey lost her temper and threw paint at him," Mrs. Marshall explained. "I have no idea why. Matthew was just telling her how good her picture was and suddenly she got mad and emptied the paint jar over him." She shook her head. "I told her to apologize, but she wouldn't. She just shouted at me and stormed off." She looked around at the classroom. "Can you help get everyone painting again?"

"Sure," Josie said, heading over toward the table where Matthew, Bailey, and two other girls had been sitting. "So, what are you painting?" she asked.

The two girls smiled gingerly.

"I'm doing patterns," said one of them, pointing to the paper in front of her.

"And I'm painting my dog," said the other. "But

now it's got some red paint on it." She pointed to a splash of red paint in the middle of the page.

"You could turn that into a ball," Josie suggested. "Does your dog like playing with balls?"

"He loves them!" said the girl, happily. "Yeah, a ball would be perfect."

Just then the door opened and Liz came in. "Lynne, I just saw Tim. He told me what happened. Where's Bailey?"

"She went to the stable with Pat," said Mrs. Marshall.

"Okay, I'll get some more help for you and then I'm going to go have a chat with her," Liz said. "She can't go around behaving like that."

She left and reappeared five minutes later with two more helpers. They took over from Josie and Anna, and the two girls followed Liz down to the stable.

Looking at Liz's grim face, Josie felt her heart sink. Bailey was in real trouble. Whatever she had done, this wasn't going to make her any happier about staying at Friendship House.

Bailey was standing in the stall petting Hope when they got there. Her face was like thunder and she was totally ignoring Pat, who was standing just inside the stall door trying to talk to her.

"Bailey," Liz said, moving into the stall. "We need to talk." Bailey looked at her but didn't move.

"Can you explain what just happened in the art room, please?" Liz persisted.

Bailey shrugged her shoulders.

"Bailey," said Liz. "Tell me what happened."

Bailey stroked Hope's neck. "It was Matthew's fault," she muttered. "He was being stupid. He said my picture was good."

Liz looked mystified. "What on earth is wrong with that?"

Bailey glared at her angrily. "But it wasn't good. It was terrible! It was dumb of him to say it was good. He only did it because . . ." Her voice trailed off and her glare deepened.

Josie frowned. What had Bailey been about to say? Why had Matthew's compliment made her so upset?

"Bailey?" Liz said.

"It doesn't matter." Bailey scowled.

Liz sighed. "Well, whatever the reason for your outburst, you're going to have to apologize to Matthew. You know that, don't you?"

"I'm not apologizing!" Bailey cried out. "Matthew shouldn't have said my painting was good when it wasn't!"

"You *will* apologize," Liz said again.

"I won't! You can't make me!"

"You're right," Liz agreed. "But I *can* forbid you to ride Hope until you do."

Josie and Anna exchanged looks of shock. No more riding? Bailey would be miserable.

"No!" Bailey exclaimed, her expression aghast as she stared at Liz. "You can't do that! Riding is the only reason I came to this stupid place!"

"Bailey—" Liz began.

"I hate it here!" Bailey shouted furiously. "I didn't want to come. I knew it would be like this. Everyone being nice to me just because . . ."

Josie stared at her. Now she understood. Bailey didn't feel shy or self-conscious. She just hated the thought of people pitying her.

"Bailey," said Liz. "No one at Friendship House would dream of being extra nice to you because of your physical challenges."

Bailey shot her a look that said she didn't believe one word.

"I'm very sorry you've been feeling that way," Liz went on. "But you are still going to have to apologize to Matthew. He was just being friendly."

"He doesn't care about being friends with me— no one here does." Bailey shot a look at Josie and Anna, and a muscle tightened in her jaw. "Hope's the only one around here who acts as if I'm normal. She's the only one who *really, truly* cares!" Picking up her walker she stomped past Liz. "You can tell me not to ride, but I'm not going to apologize— ever!"

And with that, she made her way out of the stable and headed for the house.

"So what did Liz do?" Mrs. Grace asked later that evening after Josie told her about Bailey's outburst.

"She followed her, but Bailey still wouldn't talk to her. Liz is sticking to what she said—Bailey can't ride Hope until she apologizes to Matthew," Josie explained.

Mrs. Grace sighed deeply. "Bailey was doing so well with her riding."

Josie felt like sighing, too. Bailey didn't want extra attention just because she had cerebral palsy. She wanted to be praised for things she did that were genuinely good. Unfortunately, Bailey always assumed people were praising her out of pity. A wave of guilt rushed over Josie as she thought back to the auction and how she had told Bailey it would be good to have her there so that they could see how the horses reacted to the wheelchair. No wonder she had gotten so mad. Josie felt herself turn red at the memory.

"I wish there was something I could do," Josie said after a few moments of silence.

"Maybe there is," Mrs. Grace said thoughtfully. "Bailey has started to relax around you over the last few days. Maybe you could talk to her and convince her that everyone at Friendship House genuinely wants to be her friend."

"I guess I could try—but I don't know if it'll help," Josie said hesitantly.

"Just talking to her might help, sweetie," Mrs. Grace persisted.

Josie nodded. She had to try and make things better. "I'll talk to her tomorrow," she promised.

"It might really help to get her away from Friendship House for a little while," Mrs. Grace said thoughtfully. "If she apologizes, maybe you two could go on a short ride through the woods tomorrow. She might open up."

Josie bit her lip nervously. A ride might make Bailey say she was sorry, but if she had known that Josie was going, too, she might not have been all that willing to go.

"I'll give Liz a call and tell her the plan," said Mrs. Grace. "You'll need to get a ride from Mrs. Marshall. I need to deliver the forms to the office first thing in the morning, and then I've arranged to ride Connie."

"Mrs. Marshall's not going to Friendship House tomorrow," Josie said, remembering. "She's taking Anna and Ben to see their grandmother." Then she had an idea. "I could ride over on Charity, though. She loves going to see Hope."

"Good idea," Mrs. Grace said. "But go early. It's supposed to be hot again tomorrow and it's a long ride over to Friendship House."

Josie nodded. "I'll leave bright and early—I promise."

As Josie rode along the path toward Friendship House the next morning, she was glad she had set off early. Although the sky was hazy, the sun was starting to break through and the air had a heavy, muggy feel. Josie slowed Charity to a walk and patted the horse's warm neck. Even though the horse was in great shape, Charity was already sweating and they weren't even halfway there.

"I think we should take it slow for a while," Josie told her. She looked up at the sky. There was a strange stillness in the air, and although there weren't any dark clouds in sight, Josie began to wonder if a storm were about to hit. She hoped not. She knew it was dangerous to be riding when there was lightning, and so she hoped it would stay clear.

And if there is a storm when I'm at Friendship House, she realized, with a growing sense of disappointment, I'm not going to be able to take Bailey out for a ride.

"Oh, Charity," she sighed. "I've really messed up with Bailey."

Charity's ears flicked back and forth.

"I was just trying to be friendly," Josie went on. "But I made things worse. It was so stupid of me."

Charity snorted.

Josie managed a small smile. "You still love me though, don't you, girl?" She stroked Charity's neck.

"That's the best thing about you—you always seem to love me."

Charity turned and nuzzled her leg.

Horses are wonderful, she thought. They never judge people.

It suddenly occurred to her that Bailey liked Hope as much as she did for that very reason. What had Bailey said to Liz yesterday? *Hope's the only one around here who acts as if I'm normal. She's the only one who knows who I really am.*

Josie felt a new surge of determination rush through her. She was going to make up with Bailey and show her that she really did want to be friends.

She and Charity reached the end of a field and turned in to the woods. Feeling Charity pull eagerly at the reins, Josie decided to let her trot. She still didn't want the mare to get too hot, but if there were a storm coming, then, the sooner they got to Friendship House the better.

Just as Josie reached Friendship House, dark clouds filled the sky.

We made it, Josie thought in relief as she trotted Charity down the drive and around the house.

Her relief vanished when she saw a crowd of people gathered around Hope's stall. Liz, Pat, and Tim were all there, and Josie felt her heart begin to race.

Josie rode forward toward the crowd. Hearing the sound of hooves on the gravel, the adults swung around.

"Josie," Liz said, hurrying over to meet her. "You haven't seen Bailey, have you?"

"Bailey?" Josie echoed in surprise. "No. Why?"

Liz looked pale as she said, "she's disappeared."

CHAPTER SIX

Josie stared at Liz. How could Bailey just disappear? "What are you talking about?"

"Pat went to get Bailey this morning and Bailey wasn't there," Liz explained. "I thought she might have come down to see Hope. But when we got here, Hope was missing, too. Not only that, but Bailey's walker is in the stall."

"She's taken Hope?" Josie gasped.

"That's what it looks like," said Liz. "But we don't know where and we don't know when. She could have left hours ago."

"I can help," Josie said quickly. "I can look in the woods. I'm sure Hope will whinny if she hears Charity."

Liz looked up at the darkening sky. "I don't know. It looks like a storm is coming."

"All the more reason to try and find Bailey," Josie pointed out. "If there's any lightning, I'll come straight back."

Liz hesitated for a moment. "All right," she said at last. "You probably have the best chance of finding Bailey. But, please, be careful."

"I promise," Josie said. Worried and scared, she headed toward the path that led into the woods behind Friendship House.

As she rode Charity, Josie's mind raced. Where could Bailey have taken Hope? Were they injured? If there was a storm coming, it wouldn't be good for Hope to be outside. After all, she had just recovered from pneumonia. Where were they?

"Come on, girl," Josie urged Charity. "We've got to find them!"

Charity set off at a trot, her head high and her ears pricked.

"Bailey!" Josie shouted as soon as they entered the woods. But the only sounds she heard were Charity's hooves thudding on the sun-baked ground. Josie looked around the dark woods. Think, she told herself. Where would Bailey take Hope?

She didn't have a clue.

A dripping sound made her glance up. It was starting to rain—heavy, splashing raindrops. The trees protected her and Charity a little bit, but every now and then a raindrop broke through and splashed against Josie, sending shivers up and down her bare arms.

"Bailey!" Josie called again, more desperately this time. "Hope!"

There was no reply. Reaching a fork in the path, Josie halted Charity. She didn't know where to go. Her eyes slowly scanned the ground. Suddenly she spotted a red barrette on the path to her left. Bailey had a barrette like that!

Josie's heart leaped.

"This way, girl!" she said, turning Charity down the left path. Hoping that it was Bailey's barrette and that they were going the right way, she let Charity move into a canter. The narrow path weaved in and out of the trees. Coming around a corner, Josie saw an overhanging branch and ducked just in time. She didn't know the path at all. Her heart pounded as leaves and twigs caught at her arms and her face.

And then, much to her relief, the path led out of the trees and opened into a large, grassy field.

Josie pulled Charity to a stop while she tried to decide what to do. A path led around the edge of the field and then reentered the woods. Maybe Bailey had gone that way. Charity pulled eagerly at the bit. Bending her head against the pounding rain, Josie leaned close to Charity's neck and the gray horse surged forward into a gallop.

Within minutes the reins were almost too slippery to hold and Josie's T-shirt was soaked. Her heart pounded as she tried to see through the downpour. Despite the slippery conditions, Charity raced along the field's edge. She seemed to sense the urgency.

We have to find Bailey, Josie thought desperately. If she's out in this, she's going to get soaked. Or worse.

A horrible series of images flashed through her head. Bailey hurt. Hope injured. She shuddered and tried to push the thoughts out of her mind.

Above the pounding of Charity's hooves Josie heard a low roll of thunder. Her stomach flipped over. If there was thunder, that meant there was going to be lightning, too. Suddenly the woods were the most dangerous place to be. What if Bailey were trying to find shelter under a tree?

As Charity reached a thicket of trees at the end of the field, there was a faint flash of lightning overhead. Josie brought Charity to a halt. She didn't know what to do. She'd promised to go back if there were a storm. But what if Bailey were nearby? What if she were hurt and needed help? Even though Josie wanted to find Bailey, she'd promised Liz, and it *was* dangerous to be out.

As the rain continued to come down, Josie reluctantly made up her mind. "Come on, girl. We'd better go back." Touching her heels to Charity's sides, she asked the horse to turn around, but Charity dug her hooves into the rapidly softening earth and resisted. Throwing up her head, she whinnied shrilly.

Then, faint but unmistakable, Josie heard a whinny come back to her through the rain. Hope! She would have known that whinny anywhere. Forgetting all previous thoughts of going back, she clicked her tongue and Charity trotted into the trees just as there was another, brighter, flash of lightning.

"Bailey!" Josie called, her hands sliding on the wet reins. "Bailey! Where are you?"

There was another whinny. Pulling the reins out of Josie's hands, Charity broke into a canter.

"Steady, girl," Josie gasped as Charity tried to speed down the unfamiliar path.

They turned a corner and Josie's heart jumped. They had found them. Bailey and Hope were standing on the side of the path trying to take shelter under a large oak tree. Bailey had her arm around Hope's neck and her face was very pale. Lifting her head, Hope neighed in greeting.

As Charity skidded to a halt, Josie jumped out of the saddle and onto the ground. Running over, she cried, "Bailey! Are you okay?"

Bailey nodded. "Yes," she said in a quiet voice. She looked frightened and exhausted.

A flash of lightning lit up the woods, followed by a crash of thunder. The storm was directly overhead.

"Come on!" said Josie. "We can't stay here. It isn't safe. If lightning strikes one of these trees, it could fall right on us." She looked around in desperation. She wasn't sure where to go. Going into the field wouldn't be any safer than going into the woods, because the field might get hit by lightning.

Hope snorted and pulled toward a path that branched off from the track and sloped down toward a group of low, spindly trees. Maybe that had been the best place to go, Josie thought. If they were down in the dip, they would be away from the taller trees but not out in the open.

"Let's go down there!" she said to Bailey as she pointed at the smaller trees.

"I—I can't walk any farther," Bailey whispered.

"Put your arm around me," Josie ordered, pulling the reins over Charity's head. "Try, Bailey! We have to get away from these trees!"

To her relief, Bailey didn't argue. Putting one arm around Josie's shoulders and keeping her other hand on Hope's neck, Bailey let Josie and Hope support her as they walked down the path. Hope nuzzled Bailey gently. She seemed to understand that the girl was scared and tired and needed reassurance. She pushed up close to the younger girl, supporting her weight and walking slowly so that Bailey wouldn't stumble.

Just as they reached the trees, there was a huge flash of lightning and a clap of thunder so loud it sounded as if the sky were splitting. Bailey gasped and burst into tears.

"It's okay," Josie cried above the din. "I think we'll be safe here."

Bailey looked panic-stricken. Tears mingled with the raindrops that had fallen on her face.

"It's all right," Josie said again, desperate to reassure her. "The storm will be over quickly."

"But Hope's getting soaked!" The words burst out of Bailey. "What if she gets pneumonia again? Pat told me how you thought she was going to die." She sobbed harder and hugged Hope's neck. "I'm sorry, Hope. I'm really sorry I did this to you."

For a moment, Josie was too stunned to say anything. Bailey was more worried about Hope's safety than about her own. "Don't worry," she said reassuringly, putting her arm around Bailey's shoulder and giving her a squeeze. "The storm will end. As soon as the lightning stops, we'll get her home and dry her off. She'll be fine, Bailey. I promise. We're not too far from Friendship House."

Bailey sniffed back her tears.

Josie rubbed her back. "Shhhh," she said in the same soothing tone she used when dealing with a frightened horse. "We're going to be fine."

Bailey shot her a grateful look and Josie smiled back.

The two girls huddled together with the horses as the storm raged above their heads. Just when Josie was beginning to think it was never going to end, the gaps between the thunder and lightning started to lengthen. The storm was finally passing.

As the last roll of thunder faded into the distance, the rain turned to a drizzle and finally stopped.

Josie took a deep breath. "It's over."

Bailey's arm slipped from around Hope's neck, and she slid to the ground. Hope, her gray coat soaked, bent her head and nuzzled the girl as if in concern.

Josie crouched down beside her. "Are you feeling all right?"

Bailey nodded. "I'm just tired," she whispered.

"We should head back," Josie said. "Do you want a hand?"

Bailey nodded and Josie helped her to her feet. "I'm so glad I found you," Josie said. But why did you come out into the woods?"

"I was running away," Bailey confessed, leaning

on Josie and putting her arm around Hope's neck again. "I decided I couldn't stay at Friendship House anymore. I knew Hope would help me, so I left my walker behind and put my arms around her neck. She let me use her for support and we came into the woods. Only, after we'd been going for a while I got tired and couldn't go any further. I thought about trying to go back, but my legs just didn't want to work."

"Oh, Bailey. I'm so sorry," Josie said. "Everyone's been really worried about you."

Bailey swallowed. "I'm going to be in big trouble, aren't I? Liz is going to send me home and then I'll never see Hope again." Tears welled up in her eyes again. "I don't know what I'd do! I love Hope. She's the only friend I have here."

"That's not true," Josie told her. "You've got me and Anna and my mom and Liz and Pat. Not to mention all the other kids at Friendship House who would love to be friends with you if you'd just let them. Bailey, you've got lots of friends, you just need to let them in."

Bailey stared at the ground. "Your mom's the only person who treats me like a normal person. You and all the others are just nice because you feel sorry for me."

"That is not true! Look. I'm sorry if yesterday I made it sound as if I was inviting you to the auction because of your wheelchair. I didn't mean it like that. It came out the wrong way." Josie looked closely at the younger girl. "I want to be your friend. Not because I feel *sorry* for you but because I *like* you. How could I not like you? We both love horses. We could have loads of fun together, just like Anna and I do."

Bailey nodded reluctantly. "I guess so."

"Bailey, please? Can we try to be friends?" Josie persisted.

Bailey raised her eyes to Josie's. She hesitated, but then a little smile crept over her face. "Okay."

Josie smiled at her in delight. But then she noticed that Bailey had started to shiver, and her smile faded. "We should get back. Everyone's going to be worried sick about us and you and Hope need to get dry. Do you think you can walk with Hope's help?"

Bailey shook her head. "My legs are too stiff."

Josie thought quickly. "I could go and get someone or . . ." She had an idea. "If you think you can ride Charity, I can lead you."

Bailey looked uncertain.

"Maybe I should just go get help and then come back for you." Josie said.

Bailey lifted her chin in determination. "No, I'll be fine. But I'd rather ride Hope. She's quieter than Charity."

"But she isn't wearing any tack," Josie said in a concerned tone.

"It doesn't matter," Bailey replied calmly. "I'll ride bareback. I've done it before. At my old stable, my instructor used to give me bareback lessons sometimes. She said it was good for me to feel the warmth of the horse, and it gave me a better sense of the horse's movement."

"Well, if you're sure," Josie said hesitantly.

Bailey nodded and moved closer to Hope. It was difficult for Josie to heave Bailey up onto Hope's back, but Hope stood like a statue and at last Bailey was sitting astride her back and holding on to her mane. Josie stood by Hope's head. She knew she would have to walk next to Bailey in case the girl lost her balance and needed help staying on. "Are you ready?" she asked, with Charity's reins in one hand and Hope's lead rope in the other.

Looking pale and tired, Bailey nodded, and they set off.

The two horses walked steadily along the path. Josie was relieved to see that although Hope was soaking wet, she seemed quite happy and her breathing was normal. Now that the rain had stopped, the sun was coming out again, sending bright shafts of light glimmering through the branches. The only sounds were those of the horses' hooves on the damp ground and the rainwater dripping off the trees.

After a while during which the girls walked in silence, Bailey spoke. "What . . . what if Liz sends me home?"

"I don't think she will," Josie replied carefully. "I'm sure she'll be upset, but she's going to be more relieved that you're safe." She paused. "Why? Do you want to go?"

"Not anymore," Bailey admitted. "I didn't want to come to Friendship House at first, but now I don't want to leave. I want to come to the auction with you and Anna and I want to have more lessons on Hope."

"You know, I meant what I said earlier. It's not just

Anna and I who want to be friends with you," Josie said. "The other kids want to be friends, too."

Bailey didn't reply.

Josie hesitated. Something in the girl's demeanor told her that she should watch what she said next, but she also knew that she had to tell Bailey the truth, just as she would have done if it had been Anna or Jill.

"Do you think maybe you're being too hard on everyone at Friendship House?" she asked slowly. "Think about it, Bailey. Can't you see that the other kids might actually want to be friends? That they might need friends themselves? After all, they're away from their homes, too."

Bailey shrugged. "I guess so. I never really saw it that way before."

"I'm just saying that maybe you should give the others a chance," Josie said.

Hope snorted as if she agreed, and Josie led the group on in silence.

As they walked out of the woods and into the sunny lawn of Friendship House, people came running toward them.

Liz was the first one to reach them. "Bailey! Are you okay?"

Bailey nodded. "I . . . I'm fine."

A huge look of relief crossed Liz's face. "I'm so glad you're safe. We were so worried."

The rest of the group caught up. Matthew and Katie were among them.

"Bailey!" Katie exclaimed. "You're back."

"Everyone was going crazy!" said Matthew. Suddenly, he noticed that she was riding bareback. "Hey, you're riding without a saddle! Cool! I wish I could do that!"

Josie glanced up at Bailey. Please don't snap at him, she begged silently.

To Josie's relief, Bailey just smiled. "Thanks," she said. "I . . . I'm sorry I threw paint at you yesterday, Matthew."

Matthew looked surprised. "That's okay."

Bailey shook her head stubbornly. "No, you were just trying to be nice and I was horrible. I'm really sorry and I'd like to be friends." She turned to Liz. "And I'm sorry I ran away with Hope and got everyone worried. Please don't send me home. I want to stay," she said and took a deep breath.

"We want you to stay, too," Liz said, looking both astonished and relieved. "Just please promise me you won't run away again."

"I promise," Bailey said happily. She looked at Josie and then at the big group of friends gathered around her. A smile slowly began to spread across her tired face. "I don't need to run away anymore," Bailey said. Josie breathed a huge sigh of relief. It looked as though the day were going to be bright after all.

CHAPTER
SEVEN

Liz got the two horses cooled down and into the stable, while Bailey and Josie took baths.

When Josie had dried off and put on Liz's oversized terry-cloth robe, her mom came in. Mrs. Grace was carrying a pair of jeans, a T-shirt, and a sweatshirt in her arms.

"Mom! What are you doing here?" Josie asked in surprise.

"I was worried you had gotten caught in the storm," Mrs. Grace explained. "So I called to see if you'd arrived safely. Tim filled me in on what was happening, so I came over with some dry clothes."

"Thanks," Josie said gratefully, taking the clothes from her mother.

"How's Bailey doing?" asked Mrs. Grace.

Liz, who had just appeared in the doorway, answered. "She's a bit tired, but she seems fine. I'm just glad Josie found her. I don't know what we would have done without Josie today. She's been a total star."

Mrs. Grace smiled proudly at Josie. "Well done, sweetie."

Josie blushed. "It wasn't just me. It was Charity, too. And Hope."

For the rest of the morning, there wasn't much for Josie to do. Charity and Hope were grazing happily in the field together, Bailey was asleep, and all the other children were occupied. Some were playing outside and some were in a music class with Liz.

Josie decided to use the time to clean up the stable. She swept everywhere, scrubbed the water buckets, tidied up the brush boxes, and cleaned Hope's stall. She even swept away the cobwebs from the ceiling. By lunchtime everything was neat and sparkling clean.

Clean enough even for Mom, Josie thought with a smile as she rinsed the mop she had been using. Looking around, she wondered what to do next. She settled on cleaning Hope's and Charity's tack. She had just taken the bridles apart when Matthew and Katie came down to the stable with Tim.

"Hi, there," he said, smiling at Josie. "Matthew and Katie were wondering if they could see Hope."

"She's out in the field right now," said Josie. "But I can bring her in."

"That's okay. Can we help you clean her tack instead?" asked Katie.

"Of course. There's a lot to do. I'll go and get some more sponges for you two."

Matthew and Katie chatted happily with Josie as they worked, telling her all about their music lesson that morning with Liz.

They were helping Josie put the clean saddles away when Matthew pointed toward the house. "Look, here comes Bailey!"

Katie frowned in confusion. "Who's she with?"

Josie shaded her eyes against the sun. A man and a woman were walking on either side of Bailey, who was talking excitedly with them.

"Maybe it's her parents," Josie said. The woman had dark hair cut in a bob like Bailey's and the same big eyes.

"Hi, Josie!" Bailey called out. "This is my mom and dad."

Josie went over to say hello. The woman smiled warmly at Josie. "Nice to meet you. Bailey's been telling us all about you."

"And Hope," Mr. Williams put in as he and Josie shook hands. "She sounds like one very special horse."

Josie smiled. "She is."

"Liz called my mom and dad to tell them what happened this morning," Bailey explained. "And so they wanted to come and see me. Do you think they can meet Hope?"

"Of course," Josie said. "She just needs to come in from the field. Do you want me to go out and catch her for you?"

"No, thanks. I'll do it," Bailey said. "Is her halter by the gate?"

Josie nodded.

"Come on, Mom!" Bailey said eagerly. "Watch me catch Hope!"

Josie looked on as Bailey made her way to the gate. Even though the girl's progress was slow and she had some difficulty opening the latch, her parents didn't try to help her. They let her do everything on her own.

"Hope!" Bailey called, taking the halter off the gate post. "Here, girl!"

Hope whinnied and trotted over, leaving Charity with Jack and Jill, the two donkeys.

Stretching up to rub Hope's ears, Bailey fed her a mint and then slipped the halter on. Patient as always, Hope waited while Bailey maneuvered her walker into position and then walked carefully out of the field next to Bailey. Mr. and Mrs. Williams came forward to meet her once she and the horse were out of the field. Hope nuzzled their hands affectionately.

"Come on, girl," said Bailey after a few minutes. She made sure the gate was shut and led Hope toward her stall.

"Hi, Bailey," Matthew called out in a friendly tone.

Bailey smiled at him. "Hi."

"We helped Josie clean the tack," Katie told her.

"Do you want to groom her?" Josie asked Bailey, nodding toward Hope.

"Yes, please!" Bailey said. She looked at Matthew and Katie. "Would . . . would you both help me?" she said, almost shyly.

"Definitely!" Katie replied eagerly.

Josie smiled at them. "I'll get the brush box for you."

"No, it's okay," said Bailey. "I can get it."

Before Josie could say anything, Bailey set off toward the tack room. Josie watched her go with a grin. The morning's stormy adventure certainly hadn't made Bailey any less independent!

"Bailey likes doing things on her own," Mr. Williams commented, as if reading Josie's mind. "But I'm sure you've probably noticed that by now."

Josie glanced over at him. "Yes, I have."

Bailey came back with the brush box. "Which one do we use first?" Katie asked, pointing at the various brushes lying in the box. "I've never groomed a horse before."

"You start with the curry comb," Bailey told her. "There's only two, so you and Matthew can each do a side while I do Hope's tail. You have to use a softer brush for that."

The three children began to groom. Hope snorted softly as they brushed and stroked her. She looked extremely happy to be fussed over so much.

"She's perfect," said Mrs. Williams. "She seems so patient."

"She is," Josie agreed. "She loves living here. And the children really like her. Some are scared of horses in the beginning, but after they've spent time with Hope they realize there isn't anything to be worried about. Lots of them get to ride her and they love it!"

"Riding is a great form of therapy for physically challenged children," Mrs. Williams said, her voice getting softer. "It's a shame there aren't more places that offer it. Since we moved here we've been trying to find somewhere for Bailey to ride, but there just aren't any riding schools around that are equipped with the necessary equipment *or* instructors."

"Actually, we're trying to start a riding school for kids like Bailey, here," Josie said eagerly. "My mom used to run her own riding school, so the plan is that she would run it."

"Really?" Mr. Williams asked excitedly. "That sounds wonderful!"

"I know," Josie agreed. "The only problem is, Liz doesn't have enough money to start it up. She's in the middle of applying for a grant, but the people at the town office say it could be months before they make a decision. And Liz is having some serious money issues right now. Everything seems to need repairs."

"Oh, no! That's awful." Mrs. Williams looked quickly at Mr. Williams. "Maybe you could help, darling?"

Mr. Williams nodded. "I'm a journalist for the local paper," he explained. "I could write an article on Friendship House. It would be great publicity for the riding school. If the grant department sees that people support the idea, then maybe it will help persuade them to give Liz the necessary funding."

Josie's eyes widened. "That would be amazing! Thank you!"

"No problem," grinned Mr. Williams, sounding very enthusiastic. "I'll go check with Liz and make sure it's okay. If she agrees, then I'll get my camera out of the car. It will be good to get some pictures with the article." He looked over at Bailey, Matthew, and Katie as they are groomed Hope and smiled. "And I think I know *just* the picture."

* * *

An hour later, Mr. Williams had taken about fifty pictures of Bailey, Matthew, and Katie grooming Hope, leading her around, and riding her. But Josie thought her favorite was going to be the picture of the three children hugging Hope, while the horse pricked her ears and looked straight at the camera.

"These photos should be perfect!" Mr. Williams said to Liz, who had come out to watch. "My boss is going to love this piece. I'll get the article written this evening and hopefully it will make it into this week's paper."

"I don't know how to thank you enough," Liz said to Mr. Williams as he put away his camera.

"My pleasure," replied Mr. Williams. "You do *so* much good here you deserve a little attention." Then the Williamses gave Bailey a hug and said their good-byes.

Josie thought Bailey might be upset when her parents left, but although the girl seemed a little sad at first, it didn't take long for her to cheer up. She clearly had other things on her mind. "Are we still going to the auction tomorrow?" she asked Josie.

In all the excitement, Josie had completely forgotten about the auction. "Well, yes," she told Bailey.

Bailey grinned happily. "I can't wait!"

When Josie finally got home later that evening, Mrs. Grace was in the kitchen putting out food for Basil, the family's terrier, and Millie and Rascal, Josie's two black-and-white cats. "Hello, sweetie," she said as Josie came in.

"Guess what?" Josie said excitedly as she told her mom about everything that had happened that afternoon. "Mr. Williams says that the article might even be in the paper *this* week," she finished as Millie and Rascal wound their way around Mrs. Grace's legs, purring. "Isn't that great?"

"Yes," Mrs. Grace said quietly, putting the food down. "That's wonderful news."

Josie was surprised. She thought her mom would have been much more excited by the news. "Maybe the grant people will see the article and give Liz the money sooner. Then we could really start the riding school," Josie said hopefully. That reminded her of something. "Oh, Mom, Bailey's really looking forward to the auction. You should have seen her this afternoon."

Josie's mom didn't say anything. She just started wiping the counters with a sponge, a slight frown on her face.

"Mom?" Josie prompted.

"I'm sorry, sweetie," said Mrs. Grace, putting down the sponge. "I'm just not sure whether we should go to the auction. There doesn't seem to be much point."

Josie stared at her mother. "What are you talking about?"

Mrs. Grace sighed. "Liz had some more bad news. She called me just before you got home. The contractors had another look at the roof this afternoon. They say it needs a lot more work than they originally thought and Liz is not sure she's going to be able to afford it. There is a serious chance that Friendship House might have to close."

"But it can't!" Josie said, horrified. "What about the article in the paper? Liz might get lots of donations when people read it."

"I hope so," Mrs. Grace agreed. "But there's no guarantee." She shook her head sadly. "She's very upset. I don't think we should go to the auction while things are up in the air. We'll wait and see what happens. There's another auction next month."

"But Bailey will be gone by then!" Josie exclaimed. "And she's really looking forward to it. We've got to go, Mom!"

Mrs. Grace hesitated.

"Please," she said desperately. Josie hated the thought of telling Bailey they couldn't go. "Just for a quick look."

"I guess so," Mrs. Grace admitted. "And you're right, I don't want to disappoint Bailey. We probably won't stay long. But, Josie," she looked at her, "don't get your hopes up about this newspaper article. I'm not sure whether it will be enough to save Friendship House."

Josie felt a lump rise in her throat. Her mom sounded serious. Would Friendship House really have to close?

CHAPTER EIGHT

"Are you ready, Bailey?" Josie called as she knocked on Bailey's bedroom door the next morning.

"Come in!" Bailey answered.

Josie opened the door.

Bailey was sitting on her bed brushing her hair. "Hi!" she said.

Josie smiled. Even though she was still feeling shocked from her mom's news the night before, she was determined not to let her worries spoil Bailey's day at the auction.

"My mom's waiting in the car," she said. "We're picking Anna up on the way."

"Great!" Bailey replied enthusiastically. Her

walker was beside the bed and she reached for it, pulling herself up.

Josie glanced quickly at the wheelchair beside the door. Wasn't Bailey going to use that today? It would be easier to maneuver at the auction than the walker. There were going to be lots of people there and the ground would probably be rough and uneven. Plus, they really needed to see how the horses would respond to the device.

Bailey caught Josie eyeing the wheelchair. "It's all right," she grinned, as if reading Josie's thoughts. "Even I'm not that stubborn. Can you bring my wheelchair over here, please, Josie?"

"Well . . ." Josie teased, pretending to think about it for a moment.

"Pretty please," Bailey said, her eyes twinkling. "And if you're lucky, I might even let you push me some of the time."

"How could I ever say no to that?" Josie grinned back at her.

She grabbed the wheelchair and helped Bailey ease herself into it.

"Auction—here we come!" Bailey said. Smiling, they left the room.

* * *

The auction was very busy. Horses and ponies were being trotted around grassy paddocks, while people headed toward the stables, where more horses and ponies stood in temporary, metal stalls. The warm air was filled with the smells of horses and the sounds of shouting and whinnying. Off to one side there was the sales ring, a circular, sand enclosure with an auctioneer's box at one end. People hung around the high, wooden fence, watching the horses and making bids or peering at catalogs.

Josie pushed Bailey through the crowd, her mom and Anna walking along on either side of the wheelchair.

"The ponies are being sold before the horses today," said Mrs. Grace as a beautiful bay pony was led into the sales ring. "The horses won't start being sold for another hour or so. I'm going to get a catalog. It will tell us a little something about each horse being sold and the reserve price."

"What's the reserve price?" asked Anna.

"It's a price the seller puts on the animal. It means they won't sell the horse for less than that. If there aren't any bids equal to or higher than the reserve price, then the owner takes the animal home," Mrs. Grace explained. She looked across the ring to where the catalogs were being sold. There was a long line of people. "Look, it's silly for us all to wait. If you three want to go in to the stables, I'll catch up with you when I've bought a catalog."

"Good plan," Josie said. She was ready to look at the horses.

"This is so exciting!" said Bailey as Mrs. Grace headed off to join the line.

"I like that one," said Anna, pointing to a horse cantering around an exercise ring. It was a gray Arabian with a dished face and a big stride. "It looks a little like Charity."

"He is gorgeous," Josie agreed, already wondering how much the horse would cost.

"But it's not what we're looking for," Bailey sensibly reminded them. "We need to look for horses more like Hope."

Josie had to admit that Bailey was right. Nodding in agreement, she said, "Come on, let's go to the stables!"

Once inside, they hurried toward the horses.

There was a long row of metal stalls, all with horses inside. Each stall had a number on it and a card attached to the door listing the details of the horse inside.

Josie read out loud from the card posted on the first stall she came to. "Black mare, fifteen hands high, ten years old."

Anna patted the black horse, which had come over to the door. "You seem friendly."

"But small," Josie pointed out.

"Too bad," said Anna, stroking the horse's nose. "She's really sweet."

"You're going to like all of them!" Josie teased.

Anna gave a playful smile. "I know. I wish I could take every one of them home."

Josie knew how Anna felt. But she also knew she had to be practical. "Come on," she said. "Let's keep looking."

They continued slowly down the aisle. There were young, scruffy-coated horses that looked as though they had come straight out of the field; mares and fluffy-tailed foals; older horses with drooping heads and gray muzzles; and a beautifully groomed horse with a gleaming coat and shiny mane and tail that made him look more like a show horse than a sale horse.

Unfortunately, many of the horses shied away from Bailey's wheelchair or snorted in alarm when she passed their stalls. Others eyed the metal contraption warily as they continued to munch on hay.

"For all the horses here," Anna said to Josie. "I haven't seen any that would be suitable for a place like Friendship House."

Josie nodded in agreement, her eyes following Bailey as she wheeled herself in front of different stalls. "I'm beginning to think Mom was right. She said it wouldn't be easy to find the right type of horse."

"It makes you realize how special Hope is, though," Anna said, looking around. "She really is one in a million."

Josie smiled, but, inside, her heart was sinking. It looked as though finding two horses for the new riding school would be a lot harder than she'd ever imagined.

"Look over here!" Bailey called.

Hearing Bailey's voice, Josie and Anna turned around. Bailey had wheeled herself over to two stalls in a corner. In one stall there was a skewbald horse that looked about fifteen-two hands high and in the other there was a dun horse that looked slightly smaller.

The two horses were standing with their heads over the doors, curiously sniffing at Bailey's wheelchair. Josie liked them immediately. They had kind eyes and their coats shone with health.

"I like these horses," Bailey said. "Look, it says the skewbald is named Clown and the dun is Tiptoe. They're really friendly and they don't seem bothered by my wheelchair at all."

As if to prove Bailey's point, Clown reached out and gave the handle of her chair a big, wet, lick. Then he playfully nudged Bailey with his nose. The three girls laughed.

"They're perfect," Josie said, stroking the dun mare.

"And it looks like they have been really well cared for," said Anna. "What does the card say about them?"

Bailey read the information on the horse's stalls. "Clown's twelve and Tiptoe is fourteen. They're both extremely calm and have no problems being shod, trailered, or clipped. They've competed in numerous shows and are ideal first horses."

"They sound perfect!" Josie said. "They would be totally reliable and good with nervous riders and beginners."

Just as Josie finished her thought, a woman came over to them. She had short, blond hair with flecks of gray in it, and she looked a little older than Josie's mom. Clown whinnied when he saw her. She smiled and gently patted his nose. "Are you young ladies looking for a horse?"

"Well, sort of," Josie replied.

"I own these two," the lady said. "They're wonderful." Josie knew that people who were selling horses always said things like that to try to make deals, but this lady sounded as if she genuinely meant it.

"Why do you have to sell them?" asked Anna.

"We bought them for my daughter, but she's about to start veterinary school," the lady replied, reaching over the stall door to pat one of the horses. "It didn't seem fair to just put Clown and Tiptoe out in the field, where they'll do nothing. They're both very affectionate and they need a home where they'll be given lots of attention." She sighed. "Still, it's hard for me to sell them. Joanne, my daughter, wouldn't come today. Even though we don't want to sell them, we know it's what's best." She turned away from the stalls and looked over at the girls. "Which of you is looking for a horse?"

Josie didn't know what to say. The lady seemed supernice. Josie wanted to tell her that they were looking for a horse and that they would love to buy Clown or Tiptoe, but she knew she had to be completely honest. "Well, we're not exactly looking to buy a horse today," she confessed. "We're sort of doing research to see what types of horses are available. My mom might start a riding school for physically challenged children."

The lady's eyes lit up. "That sounds like a wonderful idea. I used to do volunteer work at a stable that gave lessons to children like that. Clown and Tiptoe would be perfect for that kind of thing."

Josie stroked Tiptoe's nose. "We have to apply for a grant, so we don't know if it's definite yet," she said. "It depends on whether we get money to buy the horses and set it all up." She tried not to think about the recurring roof problems at Friendship House.

"I really wish we could buy Clown and Tiptoe," said Bailey.

"They're so sweet," Anna agreed, reaching up to smooth Clown's multicolored forelock.

Just then, Mrs. Grace appeared. "There you girls are. I was looking all over for you!"

"This is my mom," Josie explained to the woman. "Mom, this lady owns these two horses."

"Hi. I'm Helen Morris." The woman introduced herself and held out her hand. "Your daughter was just telling me about your plans for a therapeutic riding school."

Mrs. Grace shook her hand and nodded. "Yes, but it's still in the planning stage. We're not ready to buy horses yet."

"That's too bad," said Helen. "I was just telling the girls that Clown and Tiptoe would be perfect for that job. They're so gentle and quiet. They love being around people, too. Actually, the more people, the better."

"They sound wonderful," Mrs. Grace said, looking over at the horses with an expert eye. She nodded, and Josie knew her mother approved of the horses.

"I bet you wouldn't mind a few wheelchairs and walkers, would you, Clown?" Bailey said. "Or you, Tiptoe?"

"I really wish we could buy them," Anna said longingly.

"I wish you could, too," Helen said with a sad smile. She pulled a few mints out of her pocket and fed them to the horses. "I really want them to go to good homes."

As Helen continued to feed the horses mints, Mrs. Grace looked at the catalog. Josie saw a look of disappointment flash across her face.

"Well," said Mrs. Grace abruptly. "It's been nice meeting you, Mrs. Morris, but we should get going. I hope you find Clown and Tiptoe good homes. Come on, girls." She took hold of Bailey's chair and got ready to push her away.

Looking at each other in surprise, Josie and Anna said good-bye to Mrs. Morris and followed Mrs. Grace and Bailey down the aisle.

"What's wrong, Mom?" Josie asked as soon as they were out of earshot. "Didn't you like those horses?"

"I thought they were lovely—perfect, in fact," replied her mom. "Until I saw the price in the catalog."

"Were they expensive?" asked Anna.

"You could say that. Clown's price was more than I'm willing to spend on the two horses put together!"

Josie's heart sank.

"I'm not surprised," Mrs. Grace sighed. "Good horses—really good, reliable ones, don't come cheap." She managed to force a smile. "Oh, well, I guess we'll look again when we hear about the money."

And then we'll hear if Friendship House is going to have to close down, Josie thought.

A wave of despair swept over her. It wasn't fair. Why did the roof have to get a leak right now? And why did the office have to take so long to decide about the grant for the riding school? It seemed as though everything and everyone were against Friendship House. Even if everything did turn out okay, how were they going to be able to afford two horses like Clown and Tiptoe?

Josie looked at her mom. From the big frown on

her face, Josie was pretty sure she was thinking the same thing.

"Come on," said Mrs. Grace, her eyes meeting her daughter's. "Let's go home."

CHAPTER NINE

"Hey, look at this!" Mr. Grace shouted from down the hall.

Sitting in the kitchen, Josie almost dropped the piece of toast she had been eating. Her father's shout had forced her out of her thoughts about Friendship House. It had been two days since the auction and things were still looking bleak.

Her dad slapped a newspaper down in front of her with a loud thud.

On the front page was a picture of Hope being hugged by Bailey, Matthew, and Katie. "It's Mr. Williams's article!" Josie gasped.

The bold headline jumped out at her. SUPERSTAR HOPE FACES LOSING HER HOME!

Josie quickly scanned the article.

In the peaceful countryside outside Littlehaven lies a beautiful old inn, now a respite center for physically challenged children. In its friendly, warm atmosphere, the children laugh, play, and have fun, making new friends and learning new skills. Pictured above is Hope, one of the center's four-legged helpers and a big favorite with all the children. A true animal superstar, Hope patiently lets the children play around her and groom and ride her, and, according to her former owner, Josie Grace, she loves every minute of it. "Hope is so happy here," says Ms. Grace. "She loves being with the children and they love being around her."

But Hope's home is in danger of closing. With funds running low and costs increasing, the center is facing difficult financial times. Although Liz Tallant, the center's tireless manager, dreams of being given a grant to expand the center by starting a riding school for physically challenged children, the reality is very different. The office in charge of grants has months to decide on whether to allocate funding. In the meantime, the old inn is costly to maintain, and constant repairs are needed. Because it relies on private donations to keep the center running, Friendship House's days may be numbered if new funds are not found.

Josie turned the page. There, she found more pictures of Hope and the children, and quotes from some of the parents saying what a wonderful job Friendship House did. At the end of the lengthy article were the words:

Can YOU help to save Hope's home?

"Wow!" Josie exclaimed.

"Good, isn't it?" said her dad. "If anything's going to help get donations rolling in, that article should."

Josie nodded happily. "Has Mom seen it yet?"

"Nope. She's still in the shower," her dad replied.

Before she could do anything, the doorbell rang. "That must be Anna!" Josie said, jumping up. Mrs. Marshall was giving Josie a ride to Friendship House that morning. "I wonder if she's seen the paper?"

She went to the door and found Anna, Mrs. Marshall, and Ben, Anna's twin brother. Anna had a copy of the paper in her hand. "Did you see the article?" she asked excitedly.

"Yes!" Josie said, jumping up and down. "It's great, isn't it?"

"Amazing!" Anna exclaimed.

"It couldn't be better," Ben added with a grin.

Mrs. Marshall smiled as Mr. Grace came into the hall. "Morning, Rob. I take it you've seen the paper."

He nodded. "I just hope the people in charge have seen it, too. It might help speed up the grant process for the riding school."

"I wish there were some way to guarantee that the right people read the article," Mrs. Marshall said thoughtfully.

"We could mail them a copy," Josie suggested.

Anna's eyes widened. "I've got a better idea! What if we took them copies on horseback!"

Everyone stopped moving and stared at her.

"Then they'd have to do something!" said Anna, looking at them triumphantly. "We could ride right up to the offices on Hope and Charity."

Josie felt excitement building inside of her. She couldn't believe Anna had thought of such a great plan so quickly. "That's a great idea!"

"But . . . but the office is in the center of town," Mrs. Marshall protested.

"So?" Anna shrugged as if that were just a minor problem. "We can borrow a trailer from Lonsdale—I'm sure Sally wouldn't mind. Then we could park it a little ways outside town and ride up to the office with the newspaper."

"It would be pretty amazing," Ben agreed, his brown eyes lighting up. "Think of all the people who would see you guys. You could even have a banner that said *Save Friendship House*."

Josie looked at her dad and at Mrs. Marshall. It sounded completely crazy, but she thought it might just work. First, she would have to get the parents to agree.

"I guess you could do it," Mrs. Marshall said slowly. "As long as you just rode straight to the office and back to the trailer afterward."

"Sounds good," said Mr. Grace, nodding in agreement. "I'm free this morning, so I could drive the trailer."

"Let's do it!" Anna exclaimed. "You're up for it, right, Josie?"

"You bet!" Josie said, barely able to contain her eagerness.

"You'll need to check with Liz," her dad warned them quickly. "She'll have to give us permission, since we'll be using Friendship House's name."

"She'll say yes, I know she will," Anna declared confidently.

"We need to make some banners!" Josie pointed out to the group.

"And get more copies of the paper," Ben added.

"What's going on out here?" demanded Mrs. Grace, appearing on the stairs with a smile on her face.

Josie grinned. "Oh, Mom. Just wait till you hear our plan!"

Within half an hour, the plan was in action. Liz had happily agreed to the idea, so Mr. and Mrs. Grace went to get the trailer from Lonsdale Stables while Anna, Ben, and Mrs. Marshall went to Friendship House to get Hope ready. Back at home, Josie groomed Charity and got her tacked up.

"All right, girl, you've got to be extra good today," she warned the gray mare as she brushed her silver forelock. "There's going to be a lot of people and a lot of things going on. But Hope will be right next to you, so you don't need to be frightened."

Charity snorted and nuzzled Josie's hands as if to say she would be on her best behavior.

After brushing her, Josie decided to wash Charity's tail. She wanted Charity to look as beautiful as possible, since Friendship House's future depended on her. Luckily, she'd cleaned her tack the night before.

At ten-thirty, Josie's mom and dad returned with the trailer. Hope was inside and Anna was in the backseat of the car. As soon as the car stopped, she jumped out and raced over to Josie.

"Guess what?" she said breathlessly when she reached her. "Liz thinks this is such a good idea she's bringing some of the children along in the bus. Bailey wants to come, and Matthew and Katie and some of the others. Mom's making banners with them right now. They're going to meet us in the town parking lot in half an hour."

"That's great!" Josie cried.

Mr. and Mrs. Grace unbolted the trailer ramp. As they lowered it, Hope whinnied to Charity. Charity pricked up her ears and whinnied back. Calmly and quickly, Josie untied her and walked the mare into the trailer.

"Good girls," Josie said, patting them both. "We're going to have an adventure!"

Charity stamped a hoof in excitement as Hope nuzzled Josie's hand. Giving them each one last pat,

Josie climbed out through the side door and got in the car.

"All set?" Mrs. Grace asked. "All right then—let's go!"

"It's too bad Jill's away," Josie remarked as they drove toward town. "She could have ridden Faith. The horses would have loved it."

Anna nodded. "I think Ben would have liked to bring Tubber, too." Tubber was the gelding that Ben sometimes rode. "But it would have been too complicated. We would have had to make two trips with the trailer."

The truck and trailer came to a stop. Josie looked out the window at all of the people outside and felt her stomach turn over. "It's really busy, isn't it?"

"Well, there is a flea market today," Mrs. Grace reminded her. "But remember, the more people that see you, the better."

Josie was beginning to feel slightly nervous. Charity wasn't as steady as Hope. What if she got upset by the crowds?

She didn't have to worry. Although Charity's ears flicked back and forth when she clattered down the ramp, she seemed reassured by Hope's quiet presence and stood fairly still as Josie tacked her up in the open parking lot.

She and Anna were just mounting the horses when the Friendship House bus arrived. Mrs. Marshall's car followed close behind.

Ben and Mrs. Marshall jumped out. "Hey! We have so many banners!" said Ben, hurrying over. "And Liz photocopied the article so that we could hand it out to everybody. We're going to walk behind you and tell people what you're doing."

Josie looked over and saw Bailey getting out of the bus. She waved.

"Hi!" Bailey called as Pat helped her into her wheelchair. Then Pat went to help some of the other children. Bailey wheeled herself over. Hope nickered and stretched out her head in greeting and Bailey rubbed her nose. "Isn't this great? I couldn't believe it when Liz said we could all come along, too. It was such a cool idea, Anna."

Anna grinned. "What can I say? I'm a genius!"

"I guess that one brain cell in your head had to come up with a good idea sooner or later," Ben teased.

"Hey!" Anna protested. But she was too excited

to argue with her brother. "Are we ready to go?" she asked, looking around.

"Just about, I think," Josie replied. "Can I have a copy of the article, please, Ben?"

"Sure," he said, handing her one from his stack. "Good luck!"

A few minutes later, they were ready to go. Josie and Anna rode at the head of a procession made up of Mr. and Mrs. Grace, Mrs. Marshall, Ben, and the children and helpers from Friendship House. The two girls on horseback followed behind, holding banners and giving out copies of the article to curious onlookers.

Josie couldn't help thinking that it was very weird to go through the busy town on a horse. The roads around it were closed for the flea market, so there were no cars, but there were a lot of people! They all stared at the two horses. Josie was very glad she had made the effort to make Charity look as beautiful as possible. Finally, they arrived at the offices. The two gleaming, gray horses with their pure white manes and tails walked up to the building side by side.

They stopped at the bottom of the steps that led into the stone building. "This is it," said Josie, taking a deep breath and looking at Anna. "Let's go in."

Bailey wheeled herself forward to hold Hope, and Ben took hold of Charity's reins.

But before Josie and Anna could even dismount, a woman wearing a navy-blue suit came out of the door at the top of the steps. "What's going on?" she asked, looking at the crowd of people.

"We're here from Friendship House," Josie said. She dismounted and walked up the steps. "We want to see someone in the grant department so we can give them this." She handed the woman a copy of the article. "We want to make sure they know how important it is to have a riding school at Friendship House." She glanced around and everyone behind her nodded in encouragement. She noticed that even the people who had just been handed copies of the article as they were walking seemed to agree.

"I see." The woman glanced at the article and looked at the banners. "Well," she said. "I'm actually from the grant department and I'm afraid you're too late."

Josie stared at her. Too late! What did she mean? "Wh—what?" she stammered in dismay.

"We've already seen the article." The woman's

face broke into a broad smile. "In fact, we were so impressed by it that we held a special meeting this morning, and . . ." She raised her voice. "I'm happy to tell you that Friendship House's application for funding a riding school has been approved!"

"Really?" Josie gasped.

"Really," the woman replied. "So you see, that's why you're too late. The decision was already made. The money will be coming to you very soon."

A cheer broke out among the crowd and Josie's head felt light. She could hardly believe what she was hearing. The riding school was going to happen! After all her worrying, the dream was becoming a reality.

Suddenly, she realized the woman was speaking again. "Is Liz Tallant with you?"

Liz came forward. "I'm Liz."

"Hi, Liz," the woman said warmly. "I'm Sue Thomas, head of grant applications. I was going to call you this morning to let you know about the grant. Also, after reading the article in the paper, I thought you might be interested in applying for another fund we have. It provides funding to repair old buildings that are used for charitable works."

Liz stared at her. "You mean, it could pay for the roof repairs?"

Sue Thomas nodded. "Would you like me to send you over the forms?"

Liz was beaming. All of her wishes were coming true. "That would be wonderful! Thank you! Thank you so much."

Sue Thomas smiled. "My pleasure. We're always happy to help places like Friendship House. It sounds like you do a truly wonderful job there."

"She does," Josie said.

Liz turned to Josie, her eyes shining with happy tears. "Oh, Josie, I don't know how to thank you and your family. Applying for this grant was your idea in the first place and now it looks like *all* my problems might be solved."

Josie blushed. "I'm just so glad that Friendship House is going to stay open." She glanced down at the crowd that had formed at the bottom of the steps. Bailey was grinning and petting Hope, while Anna and Ben were exchanging high fives. Everyone looked ecstatic.

Yes, Josie thought. Knowing Friendship House is safe really is the best feeling of all!

CHAPTER
TEN

After the exciting adventure in town, Josie and Anna led Hope and Charity back to the stables at Friendship House. Josie couldn't stop smiling. The news was finally starting to sink in and nothing could wipe the grin off her face.

"Just think of all the changes that are going to happen," said Anna happily, as they put Hope into her stall. "Your mom's going to be so busy."

Josie thought of the things that had been listed on the application form. Besides the two new horses, they could buy new feed bins, new tack and buckets for the tack room, and a board to write the list of lessons on. "It's going to be a lot of work," she said. "But I'm sure Mom will love it."

"I wonder when she'll find the horses," said Anna. "And what they'll be like."

Josie nodded. After attending the auction, she had gotten the feeling that finding two ideal horses at the right price was going to be the hardest thing of all. "I wonder what happened to Clown and Tiptoe?" she said.

"Yeah, I hope they went to good . . ." Anna broke off. "Hang on," she said in surprise. "Isn't that their owner, Mrs. Morris, right there?" She pointed toward the field.

Josie looked over in astonishment. Anna was right. Mrs. Morris was standing by the fence, petting Jack and Jill.

They hurried over. As they approached, Mrs. Morris's face lit up in a smile of recognition. "Hi, girls. I wasn't expecting to see you two. You don't know if Liz Tallant is back yet, do you? I came to see her, but I was told she was in town. The girl who answered the door told me I was welcome to wait, so I've just been wandering around, checking it out. It certainly is a beautiful place."

Josie nodded and then said, "Liz just got back. She's in the front."

"What are you doing here?" Anna suddenly asked, unable to restrain her curiosity any longer.

The woman smiled at Anna. "I came to see if there had been any more news about the riding school. And I wanted to see if Liz would be interested in leasing Clown and Tiptoe from me."

Josie and Anna stared at Mrs. Morris in disbelief.

"So . . . so you haven't sold them yet?" Josie stammered.

"No one made the right offer," Mrs. Morris replied. "To tell you the truth, I was pretty relieved. It made me realize I'm not ready to sell them quite yet. But I've got to do something with them. Over the last few days, I've been thinking about you girls and what you said about the riding school. It occurred to me that Liz might like to lease them for the time being. I know they'd love it here and it would mean that Joanne, my daughter, could visit them when she's home from school." She shrugged. "But it depends on what Liz says. I don't know if she'll go for the idea of leasing two horses."

"I'm sure it won't be a problem!" Josie said, barely able to contain her excitement.

"Really?" Mrs. Morris asked uncertainly.

"Really!" Josie and Anna both shouted.

They were right. When Liz met Mrs. Morris and heard her offer, she was delighted, especially after Josie's mom told her that Clown and Tiptoe would be perfect for the new riding school.

"They are exactly the type of horses we're looking for," Mrs. Grace said.

"This is wonderful," Liz responded, her eyes shining. "It's so kind of you, Mrs. Morris. It'll allow us to spend money on other things we'll need."

"It's my pleasure. I want Clown and Tiptoe to have a good home," Mrs. Morris replied. "And I can tell they'll be happy here. When do you think the riding school will be up and running?"

"It depends on when the money arrives, but I'd like to get lessons started soon, while there's still some of the summer left," said Mrs. Grace. "Having the horses is the main thing. The children can ride in the field until the new ring is built."

"Clown and Tiptoe are yours as soon as you need

them," Mrs. Morris declared. "And," she said hesitantly, "if you need any volunteers, let me know. I'd love to get involved."

"We'd love your help," Mrs. Grace told her. "The more people we can get involved, the better!"

Mrs. Morris smiled at her. "Great! Then count me in!"

Josie exchanged a huge grin with Anna. What a perfect end to a perfect day!

Three weeks later, the riding school opened. The real ring wouldn't be built for another month or so, but a temporary ring had been set up on a flat part of the field. The stables had been painted and every bucket had been scrubbed. Gleaming red saddle racks and bridle hooks lined the tack-room wall and a row of helmets were hung on pegs above Mrs. Grace's new desk.

To celebrate the grand opening, Liz had put out sandwiches, chips, cookies, juice, and carrots for the horses, on a table outside. To add to the party atmosphere, Josie, Anna, and Ben had spent the morning hanging brightly colored streamers around the tack room and across the door to the stables.

"It's a good thing Hope is so quiet!" Anna said with a grin as the streamers flapped noisily in the breeze. Munching a mouthful of hay, Hope looked calmly over her stall door, her ears barely moving.

"Let's just hope Clown and Tiptoe are as well behaved," Josie replied.

"I can't wait to see them," said Ben eagerly.

"Looks like the wait is over!" Josie exclaimed suddenly. "They're here!"

Her mom, Liz, and Helen Morris were coming around the side of the house. Josie's mom was leading Clown, and Mrs. Morris was leading Tiptoe.

The two horses looked around them with interest, but seemed unfazed. At the sight of them, Hope lifted her head and whinnied curiously. Clown whinnied right back.

Anna smiled. "Looks like they're going to be friends!"

When the new horses reached the stables, they rubbed noses with Hope. Clown pricked his ears briefly at the flapping streamers but then ignored them. Tiptoe didn't notice them at all. She was too busy meeting and making friends with Hope.

"Now that the horses are here, the party can begin!" Liz declared. "I'll go and get everybody."

The patio doors at the back of the house opened and the children spilled out. Some were walking, while others came in wheelchairs or using walkers. They hurried over to the stables and the party lunch. It was turning out to be a very exciting day for everybody.

"Bailey!" Josie exclaimed, when she saw a dark-haired girl with her walker. It had been a couple of weeks since she had seen Bailey, who had gone home at the end of her two-week visit.

"Hi!" Bailey called. "Mom and Dad brought me over this morning for the party." She came straight over to Josie, her eyes shining. "I'm having a lesson tomorrow. Your mom said I could be her very first student. I'm going to come every week from now on!"

"That's wonderful!" said Josie.

"Matthew and Katie are here, too, and they're going to start lessons, too," Bailey said, looking around at the crowd of children that had formed near the horses. "Look, there's Matthew!"

Matthew was petting Clown, a huge grin on his face. Josie smiled. The two new horses seemed to be accepting the attention as happily as Hope did. It looked as though they were going to do just fine at Friendship House.

Suddenly, she noticed Bailey's dad taking photographs.

Bailey followed her gaze. "Dad's going to write another article for the paper, about the opening of the riding school and how Friendship House was saved."

"Hey, there, sweet thing," Bailey murmured, patting Hope's forehead. "I've missed you."

Hope snorted softly as if she understood.

Suddenly, there was a loud, braying noise from the field. The two donkeys were standing at the gate, tossing their heads up and down.

Anna laughed. "Jack and Jill want to be in the picture, too!"

"Why don't you go and get them?" Mrs. Grace suggested. "You can hold one and Ben can hold the other."

As Anna and Ben fetched the two donkeys, Mr. Williams came over and spoke to his daughter.

"Bailey, can you put on Hope's halter and open her door so we can see her properly, please? I'd like her to be the center of the photograph."

"Here," said Josie, reaching for the halter, which was hanging from Hope's door. She handed it to Bailey.

Opening the door, Bailey buckled up the halter and stood proudly holding Hope right in the center of the group. "Is that good?" she asked her dad.

"Perfect," he replied. "Josie, can you move in a little closer, please?"

"Here," Bailey said, handing the end of the lead rope to Josie. "You hold Hope, too."

Josie shook her head. "No, you should," she started to say, not wanting to get in the way of Bailey's and Hope's big moment.

"Go on," Bailey insisted. "Please, Josie. I really want you to. After all, the riding school *was* your idea, and," she hesitated, "well, you've been really nice to me. I never would have made friends here if it hadn't been for you. I always knew that horses made wonderful friends, but you've made me see that human friends are great, too!"

They exchanged smiles. Feeling very happy and

proud, Josie squeezed in beside Hope and Bailey.

"Is everybody ready?" asked Mr. Williams, lifting his camera. "Say *cheese*!"

"Cheese!" everyone shouted.

Mr. Williams took several pictures. "All done!" he said after about five minutes.

"In that case," Liz announced, "it's time to eat! Everybody, dig in!"

Laughing and shouting, everybody moved off toward the table.

Hope nudged Bailey as if telling her to go and join in.

"I'll take her halter off," Josie offered. "You go and snag some food before it's all gone."

"Thanks," said Bailey. She kissed Hope on the nose. "I'll be back soon, girl," she promised and then she headed off to join the others.

Watching as Bailey joined the crowd of chattering children, Josie put her arm around Hope's neck. "Well, Hope," she whispered in delight. "It all worked out, after all." Friendship House's future was safe. Josie's mom had a great job running a riding school with three gorgeous horses, and Bailey had learned that there would always be people—and horses—who wanted to be her friends. But, best of all, all of these kids had a brand-new riding school to go to—a riding school where Hope would always be loved.

Stroking the patient gray mare, Josie smiled happily. It really did look as though the future were full of hope for them all.